PENGUIN WEIRD FICTION
Claimed!

Sometime around the turn of the twentieth century, something happened, something . . . *weird*. In the dark halls of ivy-clad manors, in the ancient woodland escapes of New England, a generation of authors was inspired to radically reinterpret the horror and fantasy writing of the past. In place of vampires and werewolves were atmospheres of breathless dread, terrifying visions of long-forgotten gods and unexplainable, writhing monsters. The strange and extraordinary work from that time remains incredibly influential on all aspects of literature today. **Penguin Weird Fiction** is a celebration of the very best of this writing, a store of novels and tales that for generations have delighted and horrified.

ABOUT THE AUTHOR

Gertrude Barrows Bennett (1884–1948) was born in Minneapolis, Minnesota. Writing under the pseudonym Francis Stevens, her imaginative and adventurous tales, characterized by ancient civilizations, remarkable artefacts and fearsome supernatural beings, often blurred boundaries between fantasy, science fiction and the darker recesses of the ghost story. A pioneering female author of genre literature, her fantasy and science fiction writing was some of the first by an American woman to be widely published. Her novels *Claimed!* and *The Citadel of Fear* remain classic works of Weird Fiction.

Claimed!

GERTRUDE BARROWS BENNETT

PENGUIN BOOKS

PENGUIN BOOKS

UK | USA | Canada | Ireland | Australia
India | New Zealand | South Africa

Penguin Books is part of the Penguin Random House group of companies
whose addresses can be found at global.penguinrandomhouse.com

Penguin Random House UK,
One Embassy Gardens, 8 Viaduct Gardens, London SW11 7BW

penguin.co.uk
global.penguinrandomhouse.com

This edition published in Penguin Books 2024

001

Penguin Random House values and supports copyright.
Copyright fuels creativity, encourages diverse voices, promotes freedom
of expression and supports a vibrant culture. Thank you for purchasing
an authorized edition of this book and for respecting intellectual property
laws by not reproducing, scanning or distributing any part of it by any
means without permission. You are supporting authors and enabling
Penguin Random House to continue to publish books for everyone.
No part of this book may be used or reproduced in any manner for the
purpose of training artificial intelligence technologies or systems. In accordance
with Article 4(3) of the DSM Directive 2019/790, Penguin Random House
expressly reserves this work from the text and data mining exception

Typeset by Jouve (UK), Milton Keynes
Printed and bound in Great Britain by Clays Ltd, Elcograf S.p.A.

The authorized representative in the EEA is Penguin Random House Ireland,
Morrison Chambers, 32 Nassau Street, Dublin D02 YH68

A CIP catalogue record for this book is available from the British Library

ISBN: 978-1-405-97292-5

Penguin Random House is committed to a
sustainable future for our business, our readers
and our planet. This book is made from Forest
Stewardship Council® certified paper.

Preface

Extract from entry of May 17, 19—, in the log of the Portsmouth Bell, British merchant vessel, Captain Charles Jessamy, Master:

The floating scoria and ashes covering the sea in an almost unbroken thickness of from six to fifteen inches are greatly impeding our progress. How far we shall have to sail before we are out of the affected region I am unable to judge. With the fair breeze and all canvas set, three knots has been our best speed since meeting the seismic wave, May 14.

The port binnacle still disagrees by two and a quarter points with the starboard binnacle, and by one and a half with that in my cabin. Two of the compasses, therefore, or more likely, all three, have been in some manner affected by the submarine volcanic convulsion which caused the wave. Heavy clouds preclude observations; by dead reckoning we should have sighted Corvo early this morning. The heat is terrible, registering 150 F. in the coolest parts of the ship.

Approaching at last the island referred to on my last entry of the 16th, I determined to go ashore if possible. Shortly after six bells in the afternoon watch, being then by dead reckoning 40 degrees N., 31 degrees 15 minutes W., we dropped in a boat, and, leaving Mr Kersage in charge of the ship, with considerable difficulty made our way to land. The island proved to be perhaps five miles in circumference, being of an irregular, oval shape. The formation is a dark, chocolate-colored rock, striated with metallic-red, as I discovered by scraping away at one spot the scoria and wet ashes with which it is thickly coated.

Near the center the rock has been flung up in ridges, forming rectangular and other shapes, quaintly reminiscent of the ruins of old buildings. Though, from some distance off, I observed that in several cases the warm rain which has been falling intermittently had washed the ash away from these ridges and that the rock so bared is uniformly of the same brilliant metallic-red with which the chocolate-colored formation near the shore is streaked.

From where we stood the illusion of ruins was nearly perfect, and indeed – who knows? – we may to-day have looked upon the last surviving trace of some ancient city, flung up from the abyss that engulfed it ages before the brief history we have of the race of man began. I would have liked to investigate the 'ruins' more closely, but thought best not to attempt it.

From many fissures hot, ill-smelling, and probably poisonous vapor is still pouring up, and though the rock is sufficiently cool so that it is possible to walk on it, I deemed it safer to confine exploration to a comparatively small space near our landing-place.

I and one of the men, James Blair, were the sole members of my little exploration party actually to set foot where man has at least not set foot in untold ages, and where, in all possibility, man may never set foot again, since land of this type is quite likely to sink beneath the waves as abruptly as it rose above them.

Blair rather amused me by asking permission to carry away a keepsake of Belle Island as Kersae and I agreed to name it. Scattered over its surface are many irregular blocks and ball-shaped masses – 'bombs' as they are termed – greenish-black lava. One of the smaller of the blocks was rather pretty, having a very regular rectangular shape, and the lava deep-green in color, flecked with brilliant scales of metallic scarlet.

Blair said he meant to cut and hollow it out as a box, but when he picked it up it was so hot it burned his hands. The men who had remained in the boat, laughed, which so much annoyed Blair that he removed his shirt, wrapped the block in that, and triumphantly carried it off.

A memento of Belle Island! As I write the place is still visible, a black streak flecked with the scarlet of its 'ruins,' and set in a desolate, heaving waste of gray. I wonder if any other ship will ever sight that land? It may rise yet higher, pushed up by the mighty forces at work beneath us. Or it may be only a week – a day – till the sea reclaims its own.

I.

Mr Lutz and the Strange Sailor

'For why would I give you the seller's name? You want you should buy the thing back from him? Believe me, for that feller's name would be no good to you.'

'Naw, and I can guess why not! Why, you poor shark – you poor –'

'Now, now, mister! That's all. Speak polite, or out of my shop you go!'

Squat, square, heavy-shouldered and brute-jowled Mr Jacob Lutz appeared a poor specimen in whom to seek the traditional Hebraic noncombativeness. Looking upon him, the other man's bleak gray gaze shifted and fell.

'Slack away!' he muttered. 'I ain't huntin' trouble, and I ain't brought you none.'

With a dismissing shrug, the shopkeeper turned and began ostentatiously to flirt the dust from a crowded tableful of odds and ends. There were crudely ugly fetish bowls from the Congo, and naive wooden manikins, shaped in the half-light of a devil-devil hut in the Solomons; there was a cracked, yellowed walrus tusk, painstakingly mal-carved to represent some talented igloo-dweller's idea of a tornaq, or boulder-inhabiting she-demon; there were several greenish-black bronze Buddhas, a little badly-marred portable shrine, and various other more or less valuable oddities.

This was Mr Lutz's 'bargain-table,' set out to attract the interest of the casual customers. His 'regular people' mostly knew too much to bother with such trash.

Moving delicately to avoid oversetting a stand of Mongolian

arms that nestled a huge, bristling bronze dragon beyond the table's end, Lutz passed around the table and began working back along the other side.

'Say,' complained the man of the bleak gray eyes, 'ain't yer going to give me no lead whatever?'

Lutz flung down his duster.

'For why would I give you a lead?' he demanded impatiently. 'Yesterday morning you comes into my shop and says: "I get this here curio off a mate of mine who gets it off a Chinese steward what gets it off a Manchu that stole it from a Taoist temple. I don't know how it could be opened, and I don't know what is inside. How much you give me as she lays?"

'Right away I know somebody's lying. The writing on the top ain't Chinese. It looks like it could be archaic Hebrew, maybe; but it ain't Chinese. Just the same, you being a sailor, I think likely you come by it reasonably honest, and pay you good money. No place else could you sell for so much a curio that has no history, no name, no nothing but a pretty look and a guess for what is inside.

'Then quick I sell it again, and for more – yes, I tell you the truth, mister – for more than I pay. Why not? That is my business, and at that I ain't so wealthy. But the feller who buys it, he ain't the kind of feller that wants I should send you bothering him. He is like all my customers. They are all fine, wealthy people –'

'And I ain't fine enough to take a peep at 'em squint-eyed, eh? Well, now you listen here. I ain't got the least wish to buy back. See? Fact is, I come to do yer a favor like. After I was in here yesterday, I meets the matey I was tellin' yer about that I got the thing off in the first place. He opens up with some info I didn't have when I sold.

'Thinks I, mebbe the poor dealer will get stung, like I did when I sold fer the price of a square. I'll blow in and put him wise. Mebbe he'll slip me the half of a bum dime fer sheer gratitude; he looks like a generous slob.

'So when I find you've already sold – and fer a darn sight

more'n what yer give me, I'll bet! – I ask yer the man's name that bought it, so I can wise him up. And fer that I get treated like a dog and pretty near throwed out on my head! You give me a pain – fer a fact yer do. So-long!'

In sullen disgust the visitor jerked at his weather-beaten cap, thrust his hands deep in the pockets of disreputably ancient trousers, and slouched for the door. The dealer promptly called after him.

'Hey, mister! wait a minute. You sell me a curio and say you know nothing about it. Then back you come and say you know all about it. Looks to me like there was fishy business –'

'Sure,' flung back the other. 'Fishy-sharky business – dealin' with you, I could've told yer "fine customer" what's wrote on the bottom, and what language it's wrote in, and the whole bloomin' truth about it. But it's all off, now.'

Again he lunged toward the door.

Five minutes later Lutz was tossing down on the glass of a display case filled with carved white jades, one of his own business cards. The back bore a scribbled address.

'You give Mr Robinson that,' he instructed, 'and tell him Mr Lutz sent you. I wouldn't wonder he might give you a nice reward, can you let him know what that inscription is on the top –'

'On the bottom,' corrected the sailor.

Mr Lutz started slightly. The sailor's bleak gray eyes were fixed on him, and something in their expression – or perhaps it was a thought in his own mind – seemed to cause Mr Lutz a sudden strange uneasiness.

'But the inscription – for sure it is on the top, if you lay it down that way,' he insisted.

'On the bottom, lay it just how yer please.'

The bleak eyes held their gaze fixedly. Mr Lutz looked away hastily. Had he not been so stolid and obviously untimorous, one might have believed that Mr Lutz was frightened. Under the blueblack of his shaven jowls the skin seemed actually to whiten.

The stranger leaned to thrust his lean, brown, sneering face close to that of the dealer across the showcase.

'On the bottom, however, she lays, matey! And say' – his voice dropped to a rasping whisper – 'did yer see the white horses come in, with their red throats gapin' and the wind and the tide at their tails? Did yer?'

At the apparently senseless question, Mr Lutz drew still further away. The hint of fear in his face, however, yielded to a sudden, savage irritation. Brick red replaced the pallor, and an artery in his bull neck throbbed visibly.

'You talk foolish!' he snarled. 'Mister, get out of my shop. Go talk your foolish white horses to Mr Robinson. Maybe he's got the time to listen. I ain't!'

Some minutes after the man had left however, Mr Lutz flung down his duster and with a manner oddly distressed ran blunt fingers through his bristling black hair.

'That such foolishness I would let a feller like that put into my head!' he muttered. 'Jacob, it is time, you would take a vacation from business! You are tired out with the July heat and too much work. White horses with red throats and – Phew! – I do not like that feller! I wonder –'

He hesitated a moment, then, going to the telephone at the back of his shop, he took down the receiver and called a number.

2.

Dr Vanaman's Night Call

'I can't say that I see anything so very remarkable about it,' drawled Leilah Robinson. 'But I presume that it really is wonderful as you say, Uncle Jesse.'

'Well, then! And I suppose you can't see any queerness in the color of this here? Nor in the stuff it's made of; that surely ain't metal, nor glass, nor porcelain, nor any ordinary kind of stone? Nor in this here writing on the top, nor – Leilah, I wish to gracious you'd set down while I'm talking! You've saw all the things in this room a thousand times if once. Set, can't you?'

The young woman had been wandering up and down her uncle's study, inspecting the pictures, taking a book from a shelf and replacing it, or laying an appreciative finger on the crackled glazing of an old vase, a bit of real Satsuma. Now, her slate-gray eyes more bored than usual, she strayed languidly back to the table.

There was a box set on it – an oblong, bluish-green box, about a dozen inches long by half as many wide, highly polished, but severely simple of workmanship. Its sole decoration was a single short line of characters belonging to some foreign language, which had apparently been incised across the top with an engraver's tool and the lines filled in with scarlet enamel.

The old man, whose finger-nail slowly followed these characters, as if by doing so he might trace their meaning, was as perfect in his way as their draughtsmanship. He was a perfect specimen, that is, of the hawk or predacious type in the genus homo. It was night, and the rays of a hanging lamp brought out his face in bold lights and shadows.

The curved beak of a nose, thin-bridged and cruel, thrust out between bristling white brows. Could his face have been turned inside out, the lips might have become visible. Normally they were not, having been compressed and sucked inward till the mouth was a straight line that opened as an oblong aperture. Steel blue eyes, unspectacled and keen as a hawk's, dwelt with a curiously hungry avidity on the box and its inscription. His nails were horny, yellow claws. His thin shoulders leaned with a suggestion of hunched wing-shoulders.

Altogether, Mr J. J. Robinson did well as a hawk, but as an old man he was not quite pretty.

His lack of pulchritude, however, was not bothering Leilah. Like the things in his study, she had 'seen him a thousand times if once,' and to her he was only Uncle Jesse, her guardian since babyhood.

'It would be wonderful to use as a jewel-casket,' she observed in her silky, drawling voice.

The old hawk shook his head impatiently.

'Don't I tell ye it can't be opened? They's no catch for hinges. Nothing but this little fine hairline crack around the middle of the sides to show it's a box at all. If 'twasn't for this here red writing on the cover ye couldn't even tell which is top and which is bottom. I tried to get it open this afternoon, and the cussed penknife slipped and made a scratch – H-m! That's funny!'

'Why, I'd have took oath – Say, Leilah, cast your eye round the edge of this here. See any mars or scratches?'

He did not pass the box to her for inspection, nor did Leilah reach out to take it, She knew too well how he hated any one but himself to touch the treasures of his collecting fever, particularly while they were still newly in his possession. As he slowly turned the box around, however, held edgewise under the lamp, she looked it over as requested.

'There are no scratches,' she announced at length.

'Well, then! But I'd have swore the knife-blade made a scratch an inch long where she slipped. Are my eyes going back on me at last? Wait a jiffy,' he ordered.

He laid the box down and, rising, went into the large library, off which his study opened, for though by no means a general reader, Robinson had a splendid assortment of subjects germane to his collecting hobby. A moment later he was back with a reading-glass.

'Lutz phoned me that he was sending around the man who sold him this box,' he observed, again seating himself. 'A sailor, Lutz said, and that he was promising to let me know its real history and what the writing means. He ain't arrived yet, but –'

The old man broke off abruptly. He had been about to turn the box edgewise and search for that missing scratch under magnification of the lens; now he checked himself, scowled, and looked up at his niece with a gleam of steel-blue eyes.

'Why was you meddling with this while I was out of the room, Leilah?' he demanded angrily.

'I didn't touch the box. Why should I?' She looked at him in languid surprise.

'Well, then! But ye must have. I left it lying top uppermost. Now it's lying bottom up. Then ye say ye didn't tech it!'

'But I really did not,' drawled Leilah, the bored eyes brightening to dawning annoyance. Uncle Jesse's fussiness had been increasing of late till at times even she, toward whom he had always shown tolerance not bestowed on the rest of the world, found it hard to get on with him.

Her uncle's hawk-brows drew closer together and with a kind of half-articulate snarl he reversed the box, so that the scarlet inscription was again uppermost.

'All right! All right!' he snapped. 'But next time just you keep your hands off, Leilah. Understand?'

Making no reply to the insinuation, she turned languidly away.

'I think I'll say good night, uncle.'

'Good night,' he retorted shortly.

Leilah left him sitting there, the reading-glass gripped in one horny claw, glowering at the green box like some fierce old priest indignant over a holy relic that has been defiled by the touch of a hand not his own.

When John Vanaman, M. D. was roused shortly after twelve that night by a jingling phone at his bedside, he woke alertly, sat up willingly, and unhooked the receiver without a sign of that reluctance which work-weary physicians are prone to feel for inconveniently late night-callers.

Dr Vanaman, in fact, was not in the least work-weary. His bedside phone was a nice, shiny, new instrument, as unworn by use as the rug and other furnishings of his little consulting room and parlor below stairs, or the gleamy brass of his nameplate outside. He was as interested and inwardly excited over this midnight call as a young girl receiving her first proposal of marriage. Yet he managed to keep the quiver out of his voice and answer with steady, nay almost stern dignity.

Three minutes later, however, his pajamaed figure hurled itself out of bed with regard for haste, rather than dignity, and as he literally plunged into his clothing the faint smile on his lips might have been deemed heartless by one who had 'listened in' along the line and learned the nature of the call.

But a doctor – particularly a young doctor – is only human. That his very first patient after opening his office in Trentmont should be the richest man in town was a piece of luck welcome as unexpected. The true explanation of his being called in this hurried manner to attend old Jesse J. Robinson, owner of the great Robinson Brothers Engine Works, at Kennington-on-the-Delaware, and a millionaire thrice over, did not occur to Dr Vanaman. The romance of somewhat impetuous youth informed him that from this night on the entire Robinson menage were his patients on the recommendation of – oh, some unknown friend, perhaps, who knew how he had worked under Vincent, the great specialist at the Belmont Hospital, and what Vincent had said of him.

As he gave his rebelliously upstanding crop of reddish-brown hair some half-dozen swift subduing brush-licks, it was a pleasant, frank, inherently hopeful face that returned his gaze from the mirror. Intelligent, too, with very bright brown eyes and a mouth and chin that promised clean-cut, determinate action in circumstances of crisis. Energy, with plenty more in reserve, was expressed in every motion of his active young body.

As he had plunged into his clothes, so Dr Vanaman hurled himself downstairs and into the outer night. He had no car and he gave a thought of regret to this as he hurried along. The Robinson place, however, faced a boulevard only two blocks from his own more humble street. They might well believe that he had walked over rather than waste time getting out his car, and anyway only the butler would know whether he had motored or come on foot.

He reached the boulevard, and turned into the broad avenue leading to the house. Not wishing to arrive altogether breathless, he slackened pace.

The Robinson mansion stood well back, with a clear lawn sweep from front to boulevard. Several windows were lighted up, and Vanaman observed with surprise that one of the large windows on the ground floor was broken. Almost the entire plate-glass pane had been smashed out.

Had there been an accident? A bomb-throwing, perhaps? Over the phone a woman's voice had merely informed him that Mr Robinson needed the immediate care of a physician, and the woman had hung up before he could ask any questions.

Almost running again, Vanaman invaded the stately portico, where the front and vestibule doors both stood wide open, as if prepared for his arrival. Before he could lay finger on the bell a young woman came hurrying into the reception hall beyond. Seeing him standing there, she seemed to take his identity for granted and beckoned imperatively.

'Come in here, doctor,' she called across the hall, and straightway vanished again through some portieres at the side.

He started to remove his hat, discovered that he had left it at home, and followed the young woman. It was she, he knew, who had telephoned. The peculiar, drawling sweetness of her voice was unmistakable.

A minute later he stood in Robinson's private study, where he found the old man, clad in an elaborate Chinese embroidered dressing gown, stretched out on a lounge. As he entered, Vanaman noted that it was a window of this room which had been broken. The young woman who had met him – Miss Robinson, the old man's niece and mistress of his household she proved to be – dismissed the several agitated servants who were hovering about and gave Vanaman a clear field with his patient.

Though as yet he had hardly taken time to glance at her, subconsciously Vanaman admired the young woman's unflustered, almost languid and yet efficient manner. Experience with hospital nurses had taught him which kind of a woman could be relied on in an emergency and which could not.

A brief examination informed him that despite the ghastly lividness of his hawk-like old face, Robinson was alive, though how long he might remain so was another matter. Uneven respiration and a heavy, frantically jumping pulse told their story.

'Is it – a stroke?' asked the young woman's voice behind him.

'I don't know,' said Vanaman frankly. 'Can't tell yet. Hot-water bottles for his feet, please, and an ice pack for his head. Have you any alcohol in the house? I'm going to give him a hypodermic.'

He was directing the young woman in exactly the short, crisp sentences he would have used with a nurse, and she obeyed with equal intelligence and dedication. Soon the best treatment possible for the case was being administered, and Miss Robinson herself cleansed the old man's arm with absorbent cotton dipped in alcohol while Vanaman got his hypodermic ready. He had declined to let the patient be moved till his jumping heart should quiet a little.

'Has he had many attacks like this?' queried Vanaman, as he withdrew the hypodermic needle and pulled down a richly embroidered sleeve over the scrawny arm.

'Not any,' said Miss Robinson.

'No? I should have said – H-m! What happened here to-night?'

In his absorption in the patient Vanaman had forgotten that broken window. Now he remembered it, and also observed for the first time that one side of the room, that near the window, was in considerable disarray. A chair had been overset, the rug lay in folds as if plowed up by struggling feet, and scattered over it were many bits of shattered porcelain, remnants of a five hundred dollar Satsuma vase, though Vanaman could not know that.

'We had a thief here – I think,' said Miss Robinson. 'At about eleven o'clock I left my uncle seated beside that table. I took a book to my room with me and sat up reading. Frisby, our butler, says that at half past eleven the doorbell rang, and when he went to the door there was a man there.

'He was a rough and common-looking fellow, almost a tramp. He gave Frisby a card and said to tell my uncle he wished to see him about the green box.

'Frisby left him standing outside and carried the card to my uncle. The card is there on the table now. You can see that it is from Jacob Lutz, the curio dealer on Forest Street. I remember that my uncle said something of expecting a man whom Mr Lutz was sending around. Frisby says that my uncle seemed to hesitate, and grumbled some complaint because the man had come so late in the evening. Then he told Frisby to let him in.

'My uncle is accustomed to dealing with rough men – in spite of his age he still does a good deal of active superintending at the engine works. I don't think he was ever afraid of anything or anyone in his life, and Frisby was not surprised when he was sent away with instructions not to hang about listening. He left the stranger and my uncle alone together here in the study.

'It must have been about half an hour later when I heard Uncle Jesse shouting, and then a great smash and crash which I suppose was the window breaking. Of course I ran down-stairs at once. When I came in here –' She paused, seemed to hesitate oddly for a moment, then finished abruptly with: 'There was no one here but my uncle, and he was lying senseless on the floor.'

'And his visitor?'

'The man had tried to steal that – that green box on the table, I think. Uncle Jesse had it clasped tight in his arms when I came in.

His shouts and the noise they made in struggling over it must have frightened the thief so that he smashed out the window pane and escaped. I – can't tell you any more than that.'

Vanaman stared at her with an intentness almost rude. He was thinking of two things at once, as a man sometimes does. One thought was of amazement that he could for nearly an hour have worked with and been ably assisted by the most exquisitely beautiful woman he had ever seen, and yet scarcely have been aware of the fact until now.

She was dressed in a gown of dull-blue, with innumerable illusive, filmy folds; her hands and arms were perfectly shaped, but slender and delicate to fragility; her face had a flowerlike loveliness, and her hair was literally wonderful. Though brows and long, thick lashes were dark, her hair was almost snow-white. There was a great quantity of it, soft and fluffy and silvery as moonbeams, and it completed the delicate, exquisite fragility of her whole appearance.

Vanaman's other thought was that the exquisitely beautiful one had been on the point of telling him something and then changed her mind about it. The intelligence of a good doctor is necessarily not unlike that of a good detective. Both are born to follow obscure clues, seek out hidden meanings, and find absorbing interest in the intricate riddles provoked by the lives of their fellow-beings.

The same instinct which, used for diagnosis had won Vincent's high praise at the hospital, told Vanaman now that for all her languid manner, rather weary, slate-gray eyes, and the perfect self-possession which enabled her to tell the brief story she had related without wasting a word, Miss Robinson was suffering from an excessively high nervous tension.

Anxiety caused by her uncle's condition? Perhaps. Or it might be – What had Miss Robinson seen happen in this room of which she had started to tell him, decided not to tell him, and the memory of which caused the pupils of those gray eyes to expand so darkly when she thought of it?

'You have sent for the police, I suppose?'

She shook her head.

'My uncle wouldn't like us to do that, unless he directed it.' Seeing his involuntary look of surprise, she added with a faint smile: 'My uncle is an old man, and you know old people are allowed their peculiarities. He may even be displeased because I called you in, Dr – I beg your pardon, but I really don't know your name.'

'I am Dr Vanaman,' he said slowly, 'but how did you –'

'I asked central to give me some doctor in this neighborhood, but I only received your phone number, not your name. Our regular physician, Dr Bruce, was called out of town for an operation early in the evening.'

Vanaman was young, but by no means a fool. Inwardly he laughed at himself for the wild dream that had pictured him chosen as elect by a millionaire patient. Bruce stood at the head of his profession, at least in Tremont. He was substituting for Bruce. He turned back to the patient.

'Heart's better,' he approved, finger on pulse. 'He can be carried up-stairs soon and put to bed.'

'This box –' The young woman had moved over to the table, and indicated by a gesture – not touching it – an oblong, polished, bluish-green object which lay there. 'This box,' she said again. 'Do you notice anything – peculiar about it?'

Rather wonderingly, Vanaman came to her side and inspected the object at close range. It was about a dozen inches long by six wide and some five in thickness. It had neither hasp nor visible hinges, and a thin hairline around the exact center of the sides was the only sign by which it could be known as a box and not an oblong block of either colored porcelain or some semiprecious stone like the green onyx quarried at La Redrara, in Mexico. The top was a highly polished surface without ornament of any kind.

Not onyx, though, thought Vanaman. Instead of the regularly banded variation of hue peculiar to that stone, this had a curious, unevenly clouded effect; and if one looked long at any part of it the blue-green color of that part seemed to deepen, grow greener, and at the same time more transparent, so that presently one's vision penetrated far – far and deep. But, great God, how deep! Down – down – through miles of transparent green.

At a touch on his arm, Vanaman started violently. He blinked his eyes like a man dazzled, then laughed with a note of apology.

'The stone this is made of does affect one's vision peculiarly, doesn't it?'

Miss Robinson was frowning slightly.

'Perhaps. I haven't noticed. That was not what I meant. I – would you mind turning the box over, doctor?'

More puzzled than ever, Vanaman nevertheless complied. Then he realized that the plain, polished surface which had affected his eyes so strangely must be the bottom of the box, and that it had been lying with the top, or cover, underneath. Across the surface now brought to light was a brief inscription done in blood-red enamel.

'What do those characters mean?' demanded Miss Robinson, and now the strained tension in her voice was unmistakable.

It struck Vanaman that this first nightcall of his had brought him into touch with some situation which he did not understand, and which had some possibly very queer angles.

'I don't know what they mean,' he said gently, almost soothingly. 'I have seen an inscription in hieratic Egyptian which somewhat resembled this. But I am no palaeographist, Miss Robinson. If you wish the inscription translated, I'd suggest that you take the box to some expert in these things.'

The young woman seemed actually to shudder.

'I don't wish to take it anywhere!' she said hastily. 'I don't wish even to touch it. Not ever again!'

Before Vanaman had time to reply or question further, a sudden sound from the lounge made them both turn. Old Robinson was sitting up. From under knotted, hawklike brows his eyes stared fiercely and he was stretching toward them two yellow claws that opened and closed with grasping motion.

'Give it!' he croaked hoarsely. 'Give it – quick.'

The doctor, who had not expected his patient to rouse for some hours at least, was considerably startled. Miss Robinson, however, displayed a comprehension of her uncle's meaning so instant as to be almost uncanny. Snatching up the box which she had just expressed her disinclination to touch, she ran and fairly thrust it into his hands. They closed on it greedily. Then he sank back, clasping the thing tight to his breast.

'I got it!' he croaked. 'What I want I get, and – what I get I keep! They can't take it away from – old Jesse Robinson! Nobody – can take it! You – hear me?' His voice rose to a kind of discordant shriek, hoarse and dreadful with effort. 'Nobody can take it! Nobody! Not even – him!'

3.

The Green Invasion

Two a.m that morning found Dr John Vanaman in a place where yesterday he would have least expected to spend half the night. That is, he was ensconced in a large comfortable chair in the richly furnished bedchamber of old Jesse Robinson, the wealthiest – also some said the meanest – man in Tremont.

But if Robinson were mean, the meanness did not apply to expenditures on himself or his house. The mellow light of a shaded night lamp showed his lean, yellow, sleeping face pillowed in a bed, the cost of which would have paid Vanaman's house rent and all other expenses for some years. The elaborate brocaded silk of the curtains, the bizarre splendor of the Chinese robe flung over a chair by the bedside, were like all else in the room: very beautiful and in almost distressing contrast with the lean, ravenous hawkishness of their owner.

Dr Vanaman sighed and stirred uneasily.

He was not altogether pleased with his position. He had suggested that a nurse be sent for; and had immediately begun to learn why Miss Robinson had not called in the police without her uncle's authorization, and also a possible reason for that slightly bored weariness which seemed to be her habitual manner.

Mr Robinson, in fact, was 'difficult.' Very soon after recovering consciousness he had demanded the reason for Vanaman's presence, been surprisingly disagreeable over his niece's act in sending for a doctor at all, and then abruptly reversed his faultfinding to all but literally hurl curses at Vanaman because the young man proposed to leave him and go home.

A nurse? Never! No she-cat, whisky-guzzling nurse was going

to watch over him. His niece? No, indeed! Leilah must go straight to bed; just a little night-watching made any woman as ugly as an owl. He hated ugly people, and he would not have them around when he was sick. As for the servants, they were a stupid, addleheaded lot whom no man with the brains of a mouse would rely on.

He wanted Vanaman with him the rest of the night, and Vanaman he would have. A doctor was supposed to have some sense. Vanaman probably hadn't much, but at least he was better than the others. And there were reasons – yes, there were very good reasons indeed why he wanted somebody with sense beside him the rest of that night.

Vanaman had yielded finally, and stayed, although it was not for the amiable Jesse J. Robinson's sake. Rather, it was for Leilah's.

'You will stay, won't you?' she had pleaded, in her drawling, sweet voice. 'I – I can't tell you exactly why, but I'm afraid!'

The man who could resist that, thought Vanaman, must be less than human. Sitting there, his eyes on that really terrible old countenance on the pillow, he remembered the amazing loveliness of Leilah's face beneath its delicate crown of moonbeam hair, and wondered. How might it be that in her veins flowed even a trace of the blood of that – that hawk-thing? The silken coverlid stirred, and he knew that the old man was even in his sleep making sure that his precious box was safe. Like a child with a treasured toy, he had insisted on taking it to bed with him. What was the mystery of that box? Was there any real mystery?

Robinson had firmly declined to tell what had happened after the butler left him alone in his study with the strange tramplike visitor. Questioned tentatively by Leilah, he had grown instantly secretive in a queer, half-frightened, half-defiant way; told them that his business with the stranger was his own, not theirs, and that if they knew what was good for them they would cease to try to pry into it.

Vanaman remembered the peculiar optical effect of infinite green depths into which his vision had sickeningly plunged – till

Leilah's touch on his arm had recalled him. Leilah! A beautiful name – very, very – beautiful –

It must have been some time after this last reflection that Dr Vanaman became aware that he had slept. Moreover, he opened his eyes with an unpleasant, though still heavily drowsy consciousness that all was not well in the room about him.

Without moving his head – he was sitting in such an ideally comfortable attitude, that he hated to move – he could see his patient well enough. The hawk-faced one slept quietly. The movement of his long, easy respiration stirred the coverlid reassuringly. Nothing wrong there, but – Vanaman wondered dreamily if the weather had changed, and it was raining outside. Not that he heard any sounds of rain, but the air in the room breathed damp, as if fairly saturated with water vapor. There was a strange, chill, fresh tang to it, too, that dimly puzzled him. The very feel of the air was reminiscent of – of something familiar, but what? He was too drowsy for clear thinking.

This wouldn't do. He must rouse himself. In one way or another a very wrong condition was present about him. He fought his own inertia in the helpless, utterly futile manner peculiar to nightmare.

Without turning his head – and now he knew to his own dismay that he could not turn it, try as he would – not only the bed but the closed door leading into the outer passage was visible. And from somewhere beyond that door a sound gradually invaded his trancelike misery.

At first it seemed to come faintly, as from a very long way off, and it approached by rhythmic stages of progression and retrogression. That is, there would be a long, even rush of oncoming; then a failing and subsiding and running back of the noise till it was again almost inaudible. But Vanaman felt assured that in each time of the sound's swelling what approached came nearer than in the preceding time.

The sound had a seething, hissing quality that seemed somehow congruous with the fresh, damp tang in the air, though the doctor's numbed mind could not quite make the association and learn what either of them meant. He was not really thinking at all. He was feeling merely, and even to struggle for thought was mental agony.

The seething hiss of what approached had come very near on its last onrush – appallingly near, and Vanaman was afraid as he had never feared in his life before. But this was no normal terror. This was the frightful, willparalyzing horror of a dream. He tacitly recognized it as such, and was at the same time helpless to dissipate it by a full awakening.

From afar the hissing invader came on nearer – nearer – nearer – Vanaman's eyes were fixed in fascination on the door, and next moment he saw the dreaded thing happen. What claimed entry here needed not to open the door, nor to break it down. With the door closed, it came in under. Vanaman saw a white, frothing line appear that slid forward, curvingly at floor level, hissing as it came, with behind it a flat, polished darkness. It entered, spread out, rushed forward almost to his feet and retreated again.

He recognized the thing well enough now. He had seen it flood devouringly up and across smooth beaches where the gray-brown sand gleamed wetly and the clean salt tang of its breath filled one's lungs with life. But what was it doing here, far from its boundaries on a – yes, on the second floor of a house. He mustn't forget that.

He was sitting in the bedroom on the second floor of a house in Tremont, over fifty miles from the Atlantic shore. For the sea-tide to enter here was impossible. Gripped by a nightmarish condition, he was suffering from illusion-hallucination.

Again the frothing white line intruded and rushed forward, spreading this time from wall to wall. It had curled by over his feet, and his feet were wet and cold.

Minute after minute passed, and still the rhythmic and horribly incongruous phenomenon persisted. After its first three infloodings, the invader no longer entirely retreated beneath the door, and very soon it fell no lower on the outgo than the seated man's ankles; on the influx, green as emerald and laced with frothing foam, it was washing about his knees.

Moreover, the water seemed real; the wetness and coldness of it were chilling him to the bone. Only afterward did he recall that the sea-tide, in its common, physical phase, has certain powers not displayed by this strange similitude of it. Nothing against which it washed was stirred or floated. The brocaded bed curtains hung straight, not even swayed by the surging waves that swept past their lower edges.

A light woven reed taboret near Vanaman's chair kept its place, submerging and reemerging sedately, as if the law of specific gravity, like the law which chains the sea within its boundaries, had been suspended for this night.

And now Vanaman grew aware that with the green sea-tide something else had entered the room. He could not see it. The evidence of its presence was as yet purely intuitional. But the mere blind knowledge of its presence gripped Vanaman's soul with a terror that far surpassed his previous fear. He felt that he was dying. No agony like this could be long endured by mere human life.

And that sleeping hawk face in the bed, which had slumbered on undisturbed till now, seemed at last aware that an awful danger impended. Though the eyes did not open, the brows knotted with a writhing motion, the jaws set, and the sucked-in lips strained slightly apart, exposing the jagged yellow teeth behind.

Presently a rush of half-articulate words passed the straining lips. To Vanaman it seemed that he muttered something of 'horses,' 'white horses,' and 'the bloody throats of white horses;' but perhaps because of the water's seething and continuous noise he could make no coherent meaning of the words.

Then with frightful abruptness came the climax.

That which was in the room beneath the tide, and which had pushed the tide hither – before it, now gathered, took form, and rose up, sudden and monstrous.

Exactly what shape it had, Vanaman could not later clearly remember. He could recall only his own fear and intuitive sense of it as a thing of awful force and of a potential destructiveness terrific beyond finite comprehension.

As it rose, the green brine surged and swirled up with it in a cone-shaped, swirling mass.

The old man on the bed sat bolt upright, and as that dreadful power loomed over him his mouth opened to an oblong aperture. Out of his stringy old throat there issued forth a long, wild, bubbling shriek.

Like a knife the keen sound of it cut and drove away the intangible bonds which had held Vanaman powerless. In one leap he had sprung from his chair and flung himself recklessly between his patient and the nameless horror that threatened.

4.
The Silent Message

When man attempts a really heroic act – when he conquers fear unutterable and flings himself body and soul into the breach, bent only on protecting one he has been set to guard nor counting the cost – then though such a self-proved hero may be overwhelmed in many different ways, he can be thoroughly disconcerted in but one.

Vanaman was prepared to fight and be overwhelmed. He was not prepared to wheel defensive at Robinson's side and see nothing to combat. There, however, was the room, peaceful, silent, dry as any normal bedroom should be, and save for himself and Robinson, quite empty of anything visibly animate.

'You – dreaming – fool!' he muttered blankly, and he was addressing himself.

Again he whirled, this time toward the bed. Ah! But here was an enemy to fight indeed – an enemy old as earthly life and which Vanaman had spent years in training himself to strive against.

The old man had dropped back, his face darkly livid; there was foam on his lips, and his yellow hands, releasing the box at last, beat the air as he choked for breath. That shriek which had roused the doctor had also awakened Leilah, and an instant later she appeared in the doorway, clad in a hastily flung on negligee.

'Another seizure,' announced Vanaman; and again they were working together, two young lives giving freely of their strength and skill to save that possibly rather worthless old one.

Yet through it all, and despite his conviction that he had recently suffered from a particularly vivid dream, one question repeated itself continually in the back of the doctor's brain. What had Leilah Robinson seen in the study at the time of her uncle's first seizure, of which she could not afterward quite bring herself to speak?

The green box lay on a table by the bedside. It glowed like an enormous clouded emerald, oblong, polished – without ornament. The scarlet inscription was, as usual, underneath.

'You will, of course, call in Dr Bruce – this morning,' said Vanaman, not as one who makes a suggestion, but rather as a man who states a settled fact.

Leilah had breakfasted below stairs, and the doctor had just finished appeasing his own very healthy appetite from a tray brought to him in the patient's room. As for the patient himself, since the last attack he had slept without interruption, breathing heavily, and too deep in unconsciousness even to know that his grasping claws no longer clutched the green box, their prey.

Miss Robinson, who had been bending solicitously over him, straightened and turned to look at the young doctor, her tired, lovely eyes dilating darkly.

'You mean you can't stay with him any longer? That you don't wish to go on treating him?'

Vanaman smiled. Though professional ethics forbade him even to attempt 'pirating' another man's patient on the strength of a substitute call, to say that he did not wish to keep the case would have been decidedly untrue. He was interested in it no longer merely because Robinson was a very wealthy man. There were other reasons, one being a sense rather than a knowledge of some very queer mystery connected with it; the other and more important being Miss Robinson herself.

Nevertheless, since he was no patient-stealing quack, but an honorable gentleman, he explained his position to her and made ready for departure.

'Have Dr Bruce in as soon as you can get him,' he advised, 'and send at once for a professional nurse. I have written some instructions for her in case your uncle has another seizure, but I very much doubt if he will have one, at least for some hours. This box –'

He broke off abruptly, frowning at the translucent green thing on the table.

'Yes – and that box?' she prompted in a very low voice.

He started, and their eyes met in a long, almost challenging look. But for some obscure reason within himself Vanaman felt suddenly averse to asking the question that had been on his lips. Never mind what she had seen in the study the previous night. Let it be that he had dreamed, and that she had been disturbed by anxiety over her uncle's illness. Later, he condemned as cowardice this reluctance to have it out with her frankly then and there, but at the time the impulse toward reticence was practically irresistible.

'If he wakes and asks for the box, I should by all means give it to him,' he said in a manner almost unnaturally off-hand. 'Keep him as quiet as possible in every way, and of course if Dr Bruce is still out of town to-day and you need me, I shall be glad to return at any time.'

'Thank you. It was good of you to stay with him so long.'

But in her manner was a hint of disappointment that for the life of him Vanaman could not get out of his mind the rest of that day.

Toward evening his phone rang, and he answered it with even greater alacrity than last night. The hope that his ear might be greeted by a woman's voice, drawling and unforgettably sweet, proved a false one. But though not from Leilah Robinson, the call turned out to be both interesting and surprising.

Dr Bruce was on the wire, and after formally thanking the younger physician for attending Mr Robinson in his absence, he proceeded to the astonishing part of what he had to say. While still an intern at the Belmont, Vanaman had once met Bruce, and remembered him as a large, domineering man with a manner almost offensively cocksure and very positive.

Now he regretted the instinctive dislike he had then felt for him. In fact, as he hung up the receiver after some quarter hour of conversation, it occurred to him that Bruce must be the most amazingly generous and unselfish person in their mutual profession. And yet – Vanaman ran puzzled fingers through his crop of reddish brown hair.

Exactly what had Bruce said? He had approved Vanaman's treatment, had entered into some technical details of the old man's condition, and informed him that the patient was again normally conscious. Also that on his last call there – he had made three that day – Robinson had expressed a wish to retain young Vanaman's services as well as those of Dr Bruce. And over the phone Bruce had very cordially urged the young man 'to come in on the case.'

Of course, if Robinson wished to employ two physicians instead of one, that was nothing so extraordinary. Many wealthy men did that. What amazed Vanaman was Bruce's complacency over being asked to consult with a man so much younger and less well-tried than himself, and the fact that he seemed to be sharing his case with a cheerful generosity not only uncommon but entirely out of keeping with his character as Vanaman knew it.

However, to inspect thoroughly the mouth of this unexpected gift horse he had only to walk a couple of blocks, and Bruce had said that the old man wished to talk with him personally as soon as possible. Being hampered by no other demands on his time, Vanaman promptly put on his hat and went.

He found the old man sitting up in bed, propped by many pillows, one yellow claw caressing his inevitable companion, the green box, and with Leilah in patient, though weary-looking attendance. No professional nurse was to be seen, and for an excellent reason. The one whom Leilah had dared engage that morning had been discharged by her uncle two hours afterward.

He greeted Vanaman almost cordially, but when the young man heard the proposition he had been sent for to consider he came near rising and leaving the house incontinently. No wonder Bruce had been so complacent, and no wonder, either, that there had been that faint hint of amusement in his voice over the wire.

'You don't want me as a doctor at all,' complained the young man indignantly. 'As I understand it, you are asking me to – to come here and live, sleep near you at night, and generally take charge of you in ways that any male nurse could do as well. And Dr Bruce is to have entire control of the professional side of your case!'

The hawk brows pinched together, and the steely eyes narrowed.

'Well, then! What of it? If I'm willing to pay a doctor's price for a male nurse, is there anything to get het up over? There's reasons – right good reasons why I want just you and nobody else to stay by me a while. Treatment's a different pair of shoes. I've had Bruce for my little ailments a long time. I'm reckoning to go right on having Bruce, but I want you for something different. Ye see this here box?'

'Of course.'

'Well, then! This here box is mine. Understand? When I first seen it in Lutz's shop I wanted it, partly because it's sech a purty thing, and partly because Lutz acted kinda queer about it. Didn't seem to rightly know what it was, nor where it come from, nor even that he was right sure he wanted to sell it to me. I figgered then that somebody else had been dickerin' with him for it, and he was aimin' to run up the price between me and the other feller.

'I found out different since. I know right well now why Lutz wanted me to take it off his hands, and yet was kinda skeered to let it go.'

The old man paused to laugh. His was at all times a rather frightful laugh, a mere widening of the oblong mouth aperture, a showing of yellow fangs, and a silent writhing of the cords in his stringy neck.

Now, however, his mirth had an added ghastliness, for in it there was a kind of half-horrified, half-delighted defiance. His mouth closed suddenly and the lips drew inward.

'Well, then!' he snarled. 'What I want I get, and what I get I keep! Understand? That's old Jesse J. Robinson's motto from A to Izzard. I wanted this here box, I got this box, and' – he glanced around the room with a strange, chilled-steel daring in his keen old eyes. 'I mean to keep this box! Last night, young man, ye helped me keep it! Now do ye understand?'

'No, I don't,' said Vanaman, and glanced at Miss Robinson.

Her eyes were large and dark, and in her lap the clasped fingers of her slim hands twined nervously together. What did she so desperately fear: That her uncle's mind was going?

'Well, then, ye don't have to understand,' announced Robinson impatiently. 'Jest take it that I want somebody by me I can trust. I can trust Leilah, but I won't hev her wearin' herself all out and ugly watching by me. And I learnt last night that I can trust you. Now will ye stay by me, or won't ye? If the terms I offered don't suit, come right out and say so. Ye'll find old Jesse Robinson can afford to pay –'

'The terms are fair enough,' interposed Vanaman. 'It isn't that.'

With pointblank refusal on his tongue, he looked again at Miss Robinson, and wavered. Unspeaking, the silent, desperate appeal in her eyes was unmistakable.

Vanaman was no vain fool to fancy that the young woman had succumbed on such short acquaintance to his personal attractions and wished him in the house for that reason. No; she was, for some cause, suffering torments of fear, all the more pitiable because of the tense self-control that allowed only a glimpse of her inward terror to look forth ever and again.

Wordlessly she claimed protection from – exactly what he knew not. But he did know that she claimed it of him, Vanaman, and that he had been hesitating on a point of personal pride!

'If ye have to do it, ye could attend to your practice from this house daytimes,' began the old man grudgingly, 'but nights –'

'My practice is not in existence as yet,' broke in the doctor, and smiled. No one, looking at his frank, suddenly cheerful face, would have dreamed that he that moment decided to offer up a heroic sacrifice, let all his ambitious hopes go a-glimmering for a time, and accept a service that would humiliate him in the eyes of every other physician in town who might learn of it.

'I only opened my office in Tremont three days ago,' he explained. 'When do you wish my – ah – attendance to begin, Mr Robinson?'

'To-night – now. Can't tell what minute I might need ye.'

'Very well. And I can assure you,' said Vanaman, speaking rather slowly, like a man who wishes to give full weight to each word, 'that for whatever reason I am needed here, you can rely on me to the full extent of my ability and power to help.'

'Think I'd be wanting ye if I didn't know that?' grumbled Robinson, snarling and testy.

But – the doctor in speaking had looked toward Leilah, not him, and the silent gratitude and relief in a pair of slate-gray eyes had already made of his offered sacrifice a holy and a beautiful thing.

5.

The Sinking Inscription

Three days later Dr Vanaman walked into the roomy library of the Robinson house, set something he carried on the reading table, and with smiling lips, but almost sternly serious glance looked across it to the gracefully languid young lady who occupied a corner of the broad window seat.

'Miss Robinson,' he said, 'I believe that you and I have a very unusual problem here – and that it is time we at least attempt to begin solving it. Do you agree with me?'

At the blunt question the woman paled slightly; but three days had been ample for Vanaman to learn the tempered steel which underlay her apparent fragility. Where she showed faint signs of fear, many another woman would have been hysterically panic-stricken, and under that silksoft mass of moonlight hair was a remarkably clear and well-ordered mind. She kept all her uncle's personal accounts, ran his household smoothly as clockwork, and was the only one of his relatives who would on any terms consent to live with him.

Vanaman had heard that fact from the old man's own snarling mouth; while from Leilah, not in complaint, but as explanation of certain conditions, he had learned a bit more: That her uncle had never approved of her either entertaining or going out much; that he liked her near him a great deal of the time; and that in consequence she had practically no friends of her own age.

She feared he, Dr Vanaman, would find living in her uncle's house a 'trifle lonely and tedious at times.' Lonely and tedious! Ye gods, thought Vanaman. Here was a sprite of the moonlight harnessed to a task fit for trying a medieval saint's grim patience.

Under the lash of old Robinson's continual petty and tyrannical faultfinding, he had already found his own self-control strained to the uttermost; and added to that strain was the unique and somewhat appalling problem to which he had just now referred.

The woman rose and came across the room. They stood with the table between them, both eying with a curiously fascinated attention the thing he had laid down there.

It glowed, that thing – vivid, beautiful like an enormous, clouded emerald with spaces of translucent green into which the vision might sickeningly plunge to unbelievable depths. But the scarlet inscription could not be seen, for it was beneath as the box lay on the table.

After a moment Vanaman wrenched his eyes from it, looked up and smiled. There was courage and reassurance in his glance, and the woman's sensitive face brightened.

'First,' said the young doctor, 'let us both admit that we have been and are afraid! After that perhaps we can face our problem, analyze it, and discover that what we are afraid of is empty of real cause for terror as a dream. That last, in fact, is my present theory.'

'That the nightly horror which visits this house is a dream?' whispered the woman. 'But how could three of us –'

'An induced dream,' he broke in. 'A kind of a dream which might better be termed hallucination, perhaps, but a dream none the less, and only dangerous if the dreamers permit themselves to accept illusion as material fact. I'll more fully explain what I mean later. Before we formulate any definite hypothesis, suppose we compare notes, Miss Robinson, and set out what real, unquestionable facts we have in due order.'

The woman seemed to hesitate, frowning at the glowing greenness whose incredible riddle Vanaman had asked her help in solving.

'I am willing,' she said at length. 'But – would you consider me very silly and timorous if I asked you to put that box away in some other room while we talk of it?'

He smiled at her again, rather grimly this time.

'I don't like it myself,' he admitted, 'but I have given my solemn word of honor, not to let it out of my sight until your uncle returns. You knew that he had gone out?'

'Oh, yes. There is trouble over at the plant. The engine works at Kennington are very close to the river, and the high water that resulted from Thursday's storm has flooded part of the main building. They have had the same trouble two or three times in past years, but always in the spring. A flood in July – is rather strange, don't you think?'

'Not strange following a storm like yesterday's,' asserted Vanaman, with considerable firmness.

'Very well. I shall try to think it is not strange, then. Anyway, I endeavored to dissuade Uncle Jesse from going there, but failed. He said that Dr Bruce had pronounced him fit to be out of bed, that he was needed at the works, and that nobody and no thing' – she glanced meaningly at the box – 'should keep him from superintending his own property as long as he had strength to do it.'

'Your uncle has a remarkably strong will,' conceded the doctor. 'And now shall we table our cards?'

'I am ready.'

The woman sank into a chair, and Vanaman drew up one opposite. His matter-of-fact manner was deliberate and sustained, not only for the woman's sake but his own. That horror to which she had referred as visiting this house each night had come perilously near to shaking, if not actually breaking his will to go on facing it.

Dread of the supernatural was a form of cowardice he had never expected to have to combat in himself. Meeting it, he was resolutely determined not to yield, and for that reason was bent on lifting consideration of the affair from the emotional region where dwells animal panic, to the intellectual, where fear is only recognized as a symptom, and its causes as but fit subjects for cold analyzation and a probing after immutable law behind.

'First,' began the doctor, 'are you willing to describe exactly what condition you found in Mr Robinson's study that first night when you sent for me?'

'I'll try. I would have told you then, only I was afraid.'

'That the story would cast suspicion on your mental balance? You were quite right. We devotees of science are too ready to bestow that sort of aspersion on the witness of unusual phenomena. But my education has broadened remarkably since then. You are entirely safe now, Miss Robinson. Tell me that you saw the tail of the world serpent, Midgard, just whisking out through the broken window, and I'll meet your statement with tolerance and belief!'

He had exaggerated lightly, meaning to give the woman confidence; but the words were sooner out than he experienced a sickening wonder. Why had he cited that particular prodigy for his example of the hard-to-believe?

In the old Norse mythology Midgard, the serpent that girdles the world, is none other than the sea – the green, hissing, marauding, and claimant sea.

Almost savagely he thrust thought of it from him and forced his attention back to the woman.

'What first frightened me,' she was saying, 'was the inexplicable quality of it all. I couldn't understand. I came running through the library here, and the study door was open. As I drew near to it I had a sudden queer conviction that I was running through dense, wet mist. I don't mean that any mist was visible. The air seemed quite clear to look through. But it breathed and felt damply chilly, just as one notices it at sea when the steamer plunges into a fog-bank. Then I reached the doorway –'

She paused.

'Well?'

'My uncle was lying in a huddled heap, and – and there was something wide and flat and dark in the room. It overspread all the floor, except near the window where Uncle Jesse lay, and when I came in it went back. It slid away back toward the far wall with a kind of hissing, seething noise. You know what I mean?'

'Yes, I do,' said Vanaman, his face rather white.

'I ran to my uncle. He was huddled face down, crouched over something he had his arms clenched tight around, as if to protect it. He relaxed when I touched him. Then Frisby and some of the other servants came running in and they lifted Uncle Jesse to the couch. Hardly knowing what I was about, I picked up the – the box. Then – I had been frightened before, but the instant I had the box in my hands I was worse than frightened. I was sick – literally sick with fear. It wasn't a matter of knowing or thinking, doctor. It was just fear, blind and unreasoning.'

'I know that, too,' he nodded grimly.

'Somehow I must have set the box on the table without dropping it, and next I knew I heard my own voice giving some directions to the servants. My voice sounded so quiet and calm that it almost shocked me. And in the general excitement no one, evidently, had noticed anything odd in my manner. That is all I have to tell. You know the rest.'

'May I ask one question?'

'As many as you like, certainly.'

'Three subsequent nights since that first time, I have been beside your uncle when what comes here invaded his bedroom. Twice you flashed in from your own room while the cry for help was still on his lips. What did you see then?'

'I saw' – her voice was a strained whisper – 'water – green water that whirled upward – and rising out of it –'

'Never mind!' The exclamation was so sharp and harsh that Vanaman himself started, then leaned back in his chair, pale to the lips and with a shamed, miserable look in his bright brown eyes.

'I beg your pardon, Miss Robinson, You were merely answering my question. Will you please forgive that extremely rude interruption, and finish?'

But the woman shook her head.

'I was forcing myself to describe something of which the very thought is an unendurable terror. It is very evident that we have both seen the same thing. Suppose we leave describing it in words for another time.'

'What an utter coward you must think me!'

She leaned toward him, the delicate color in her cheeks deepening to warm rose.

'Dr Vanaman, if you were a coward, the first night you spent in this house would have been the last! But you have had four nights and three days of Uncle Jesse, and – this other, and I doubt if you've slept eight hours in the whole time. You are worn out. No, I don't consider you a coward. I think you are a very brave man!'

Her languid manner had fallen away like a veil, revealing for one instant the clear, bright soul that dwelt repressed behind it. Vanaman drew a deep breath, threw back his shoulders, and sat straight again.

'Thank you!' Though brief, the acknowledgement sounded uncommonly deeply meant. 'After that, I believe I really am brave enough to try a little experiment that the coward in me has been putting off on one pretext or another. Do you mind?'

Deliberately he took the box in his hands, reversed it, and set it down again. The scarlet inscription lay across it as if written in characters of blood.

'Will you help me watch?' he asked quietly.

'You mean –'

'I have observed a rather curious trait in that inscription. It has a retiring disposition. One lays the box down top uppermost, turns around, and a minute later, perhaps, turns back to find that the inscription has again – retired. I don't really believe that the box is alive and turns itself over. All material objects are subject to material law. That is axiomatic. Certain hallucinations of a more or less illusive character appear to follow the presence of this box; but the box itself is, by all evidence of the senses, a material object. Hence, material law must govern the behavior of its inscription. Will you help keep it under observation for a time?'

The woman nodded silently, and for several minutes the two kept their eyes firmly fixed on the scarlet characters. Nothing happened.

'I am convinced,' said Vanaman, without relaxing his vigilant observation, 'that if your uncle cared to take us into his confidence, he could unravel the whole mystery, whatever it is. I believe that he learned the truth from the man who called on him that first night – the one from whom Lutz obtained the box – and who for reasons of his own left in haste, taking the window-pane with him.

'I tell you frankly, Miss Robinson, that your uncle is the most unusual person I have ever met. He seems not in the least afraid as we are. Though the statement sounds preposterous, I should say that in some fierce, strange, incomprehensible way of his own he is actually enjoying his possession of this box. Assuming that it has valuable contents, one could understand that. But he claims neither to know nor care what it contains.

'When I suggested that he have it forced or broken open, he was very angry, called me a – well, he was angry. He occasionally refers to some person or persons who would rob him of the box if might be. But he never mentions them by name. Merely as "he" or "they." And he seems to take that fierce, gloating pleasure I spoke of in merely keeping the box from them.'

The woman sighed.

'My uncle is an old man, Dr Vanaman,' she said gently. 'With some people I think that lifelong peculiarities are inclined to become almost mania in old age. Uncle Jesse has always been very determined about acquiring or achieving anything he sets his mind on. About ten years ago he took up his collecting hobby. He began with antique coins, but as time passed he would buy anything – pictures, porcelain, ivories, tapestries – anything at all odd or beautiful and particularly anything that other collectors cared about.

'Once, when I was a child of twelve, he took me to Paris with him. We went in great haste, and I didn't know why till he came into the hotel where we were stopping and showed me a little terra-cotta figurine. It was one that had been dug up from the ruins in Assyria, and it seems was quite famous. Hearing that it was to be offered for sale, several wealthy American collectors had cabled their Paris agents to bid for it; but Uncle Jesse was the only one who went after it in person.

'We came straight home, and afterward uncle seemed greatly annoyed because only one man tried in turn to buy the figurine from him. It was not that he wished to make money by selling it again; but he appears to take that strange, fierce joy you spoke of in merely possessing something that other people want. I am afraid his chief pleasure in collecting is just that.'

'And – now – now he has a box, and values –'

'Values it because some other person wants it. I see.'

'Dr Vanaman,' her voice again lowered tensely, 'is it some person he is holding the box from – or some things?'

'Perhaps actually from neither. As I said in the beginning, I have a theory about this affair; a theory based on other alleged phenomena of illusion in which, to be frank, I have never previously had any belief whatever. But a man who won't change his views on any terms is merely stupid. We have two alternatives. We can accept the peculiar phenomena we have both witnessed as demonstrations of the rankly, outrageously supernatural. I prefer not to do that. It would mean – Well, I prefer not to do it. The other alternative diverges from material law as defined by science, but not so acutely. You know the meaning of the word psychometry?'

She shook her head.

'It is a word coined by spiritualists to express a power claimed by some mediums. A given object is placed in the hands of the medium, and from contact with that object he or she is enabled to describe events, persons, and scenes germane to the object's past history. For a hypothetical case, let us suppose that the medium is given the terra-cotta figurine your uncle bought in Paris. Blindfolded, without knowing what the object is, the medium is expected to visualize scenes in ancient Assyria which originally surrounded the figurine.

'In other words, every material object of fixed form is assumed to retain an impression of all its previous surroundings; a psychic, not a physical impression, but one which enables a so-called "sensitive" to read of its history like a book.'

'You mean that in the history of this box –' She paused, hesitating.

'That in its history,' he supplemented, 'is some terrific event connected with the box and that at certain periods, regulated God knows how, people who are near the box or in contact with it suffer an illusion which represents the event. And the theory has one advantage. There is a bare chance that we can prove it.'

'But how?'

'I have two ways in mind. One is to get in touch ourselves with the stranger whom Mr Lutz sent around here.'

Assenting, the woman left Vanaman to watch alone over his queer charge while she sought the phone in her uncle's study. A few minutes later she returned.

'Mr Lutz is out of town,' she announced disappointedly. 'He left the shop in care of an assistant, and has gone away for some weeks. I talked with the assistant, but he didn't seem to know exactly when Mr Lutz would return, nor even where he could be reached by letter. That he is taking a vacation "somewhere at the shore" was all I could find out.'

'Humph! Lutz must have wanted to disattach himself pretty fully from business if he left no mailing address. Well, that road is indefinitely blocked, then. There remains the second way, which I should have preferred not to use. Since this box is really your uncle's property, and I have no right to take it out of the house, I shall write to New York and ask a certain person to come on to Tremont.'

Forgetfully, they both had allowed their eyes to stray from the box to one another's faces. Yet Vanaman was entirely sure that neither he nor the woman had touched it, and even admitting that it had some miraculous power to lift and reverse itself, such an evolution could not possibly have been performed without attracting their attention.

The box, nevertheless, now presented only its polished, unornamented surface to their bewildered vision. Following its usual uncanny preference, the scarlet inscription had again retired, and on gingerly investigating Vanaman found it on the bottom.

'That's enough!' ejaculated the doctor, rising suddenly. 'There is your uncle's car coming up the drive. I'm going to turn his precious box over to him and tell him that he can either allow me a couple of hours to get out of this house and relax, or accept my resignation!'

6.

White Horses

NOVEL EXCITEMENT ON ATLANTIC CITY BEACH. INSANE MAN FRIGHTENS EARLY MORNING CROWD, THEN LEAPS FROM PIER — IDENTITY OF SUICIDE UNDISCOVERED.

(Atlantic City, July 24.)

At 8 a.m. this morning a man appeared walking up the beach from the direction of the inlet. He was leading a horse by a halter, and attracted some attention because of the animal's beauty. It was snow-white, and apparently a thoroughbred. The board walk was unusually thronged for that hour. Many had come out to view the effect of last night's unseasonable storm, and while most of these early risers kept to the board walk, a few were on the beach, and among them two lifeguards.

When the man leading this horse encountered the pair of guards, one of them, Jimmy Dolan, accosted him and, in a joking way, asked if he meant to give the horse a swim. The man, who was well dressed but hatless, splashed with mud, and, according to Dolan, rather wild-eyed, made a muttered reply, in which the guards could distinguish only some reference to an 'archangel,' and passed on. Suspicious, Dolan turned and followed him.

A few yards further along the man halted, and drew something from under his coat. Dolan caught the flash of steel, saw that it was a knife, and jumped for him. The maniac made a slash at Dolan, missed him, and cut a gash in the horse's neck, when the spirited animal plunged, and, wrenching away its halter, made off at a gallop along the beach. With a shriek the lunatic started to pursue, but when Dolan again attempted to seize him, he evaded the guard and dashed up a near-by flight of steps to the board walk. The crowd made way before his wildly brandished knife, and, turning, he vaulted the low gate-railing of Clancy's Recreation Pier, rushed out to the end of the pier, where another low rail fronts the open water, and springing upon it with a mad yell, flung himself headlong into the sea. Though guards put out a boat immediately, it was impossible to save him.

SPECIAL EXTRA!

(Tremont, July 25.)

The insane man who committed suicide by springing from Claney's Pier in Atlantic City has been identified as in all probability Mr Jacob Lutz of this city, who disappeared Tuesday, July 15, and whose family and friends have been since vainly trying to trace his whereabouts. While the body has not been recovered, Mr Sam Trimble, owner of a farm near Absecon, New Jersey, has come forward with information. Yesterday afternoon, it seems, a well-dressed man visited his farm, and said that he understood Trimble had a white horse he wished to sell. This was true, but the horse was a blooded animal. Mirror, out of Sunlight, by Chalmers III, and Trimble wanted a higher price than the stranger wanted to pay.

In the end, he induced Trimble to knock off five hundred dollars, and made an immediate payment of the remaining three thousand in bills of large denomination, which he seemed to have with him for that purpose. He also gave Trimble his business card, showing him to be Jacob Lutz, the curio dealer, whose store is at No. 901 Forest Street, in Tremont.

It was then nearly night, but to Trimble's surprise Mr Lutz insisted on leading the horse away with him. He had come on foot, and when Trimble last saw him he was going toward Absecon. How he made the journey from Absecon to Atlantic is not known. He had told Trimble that he did not know how to ride, and that it was no use putting a saddle on Mirror, as he would be afraid to mount him.

When seen on the beach this morning, both horse and man were liberally splashed with marsh-mud, and it is supposed that the unfortunate Mr Lutz, in a fit of temporary insanity, had somehow managed to make his way through the storm on foot across the swamps, waterways, and bridges from Absecon to Atlantic.

Mr Lutz was well and favorably known in Tremont, and it is with deep regret –

Having read thus far in the late extra of the Tremont Inquirer, Dr Vanaman returned hastily to the beginning and read it all through over again. This was the first paper he had seen that day, and old Robinson, who had been perusing it throughout luncheon, had just tossed it to him with a kind of malicious grin and passed on out of the dining-room, leaving his niece and the doctor to make what they might of the news. That it had some bearing on the uncanny mystery of the green casket, Vanaman was sure as if Robinson had told him so in words, instead of merely casting him that malicious leer along with the paper.

Another nerve-racking night had passed since his conversation with Leilah in the library. The strain of those weirdly dreadful invasions was telling far more heavily on the young man than on old Robinson himself. After that first night, the latter had suffered no more seizures of the sort that caused Leilah to call in Dr Vanaman. Between darkness and dawn each night the illusion, or hallucination, or phantom of the green sea-tide would invade his sleeping-chamber; last night the phenomenon had recurred three times within eight hours.

But though at each climax, when the phantom waters swirled up in a frothing mass and the supreme terror threatened, Robinson would awaken and shout vociferously for help, he no longer lost consciousness afterward nor failed to sleep with enviable soundness through the peaceful interims.

With Vanaman the case was maddeningly different. Hours he would lie awake, every nerve on edge, waiting, expectant. Then sudden sleep would catch him unawares, and he would awaken perhaps a bare half hour later to the trancelike horror of fear which he could by no effort escape till Robinson's voice shrieked his name, and he would leap, as if galvanized, to the rescue.

That the frightened vision vanished instantly thereafter was some consolation, but hardly enough to make him in love with his task.

Only one consideration, in fact, lent Vanaman the courage and endurance to go on. He was very positive that should he desert, Leilah would be called to take his place as watchman. As it was, she always roused when her uncle called, but at least she did not have to sit or lie in that room and endure the waking nightmare which preceded the shrill alarm.

And now this shocking news of Lutz. Vanaman had a reason of his own, which he did not impart to Leilah, for associating the white horse episode with their own problem, When she in turn had read of the dealer's suicide and the singular actions that preceded it, the doctor was relieved to see that, though shocked, the woman seemed to accept the newspaper account at face value. That the obvious insanity of Lutz had led him to involve a white horse in the details of his tragic end meant nothing to her, and Vanaman was glad, very glad that it did not.

If she lacked the necessary knowledge, or if, having that knowledge, her mind had failed to make the association his had leaped to, then by all means let her remain ignorant. There was dismay enough for her in the situation without the added horror of guessing why Lutz had bought the white horse.

Hope of tracing the original owner of the green box through the dealer was now, of course, definitely ended. Vanaman had, however, written to the person in New York whose presence in Tremont was necessary to the success of that second plan, of which he had spoken vaguely to Leilah, and had also mailed a carefully traced facsimile of the scarlet inscription to an acquaintance of his, Professor Bowers Shelbach.

The latter gentleman, if any one, should be able to give him a translation. Though but a few years older than Vanaman, Shelbach was a linguist and archeologist of considerable fame. The doctor had made his acquaintance in college days and the two had become sufficiently intimate to warrant this claim on the young professor's erudition.

Till he should receive replies to these letters, however, there seemed no more he could do, save endure, and for the alleviation of that misery he had the growing though rather dangerous joy of Leilah's companionship.

Vanaman was trying very hard to keep his feeling for the woman within the bounds of friendship. The Robinson millions stood between, and he must keep within those bounds, or be judged a fortune-hunter. But even in what he sternly termed friendship her mere presence was a delight, and the continual humiliation of Robinson's snarling tyranny was robbed of half its sting by her comradeship.

One thing he had made up his mind to. Sold into practical slavery as he found himself, at least an hour or so each day must be his own to get away from Robinson's house, from Robinson's self, and from Robinson's darling treasure, the green box. Yesterday his announcement to this effect had been very unpleasantly received, and though he had ended by simply putting on his hat and going, all through the long, energetic tramp he took, his ears had burned with memory of certain terms applied to himself in Leilah's presence for which he would have soundly thrashed any other man than her uncle.

To-day, however, greatly to his surprise, shortly after luncheon the old man not only reminded him almost courteously that a couple of hours off duty were due him, but actually suggested that Leilah also might be the better for an airing.

"'Tain't jest any young chap I'd let Leilah go round with alone,' he said, with his usual blunt crudeness. 'But I reckon she's right safe with you, and I don't need either one of ye round me for a while. Course, if you've got any business to tend to, doctor, and don't want the gal along –'

'I shall be delighted – deeply, very deeply honored if Miss Robinson will accept my escort,' broke in Vanaman, red to the ears.

The woman's face, not unnaturally, had also assumed a lovely but painful shade of crimson; but as their eyes met, the humorous aspect of the situation struck them both, and embarrassment passed in a silent flash of amusement. Robinson's keen glance was fixed on his precious box, not them, and he continued, apparently unaware that he had created any embarrassment to be relieved:

'If ye want to, ye can take out the roadster, Leilah. But don't run her over that new road they're laying – beyond the park, like ye did last time. Mind. I don't grudge ye the use of the car, Leilah, but we ought to have some sense and remember that new macadam is hard on the tire-casings. And don't –'

'If Dr Vanaman is willing, I should prefer walking to taking out the car,' interposed Leilah.

'Suit yourselves,' grumbled her amiable relative. 'But don't neither of ye go round saying I treat my own flesh and blood mean, and make ye foot it to save the price of gasoline. I ain't mean, only I like what I own to be took care of.'

'You have never been mean to me, uncle,' assured Leilah, and quite amazingly to Vanaman, the woman bent for a brief moment over the stooped, hawklike old tyrant and kissed him.

Later, as they strolled rather aimlessly up the boulevard, she said quietly:

'Uncle Jesse has always been very good to me, Dr Vanaman. If he is a little trying at times, and I seem impatient, you mustn't misunderstand.'

'When the time comes that I see you impatient under any circumstances I'll try not to misunderstand,' the doctor retorted rather grimly.

'Oh, but I often am,' laughed the woman. 'Really, I have my own large share of the Robinson temper, and I sometimes think it has been very good for me to live with a person who is a trifle unreasonable occasionally; I've acquired a fair amount of self-control. Shall we turn into the River Drive? It's very pretty along here.'

They did, and it was, as she said, very pretty, for the trees arched above it tunnel-like, and to the right rolled the Delaware, darkly aflash, like polished steel in the slanting sunlight. Just now the broad current was anomalously flowing up-stream, for the Delaware knows the sea and her sullen waters are brackish and controlled by his tides many miles from the coast.

'The river is still very high,' observed the woman presently.

'It is the inflowing tide,' said Vanaman; then wished he had not spoken, or that they had not come to walk by the river.

By tacit consent, they had avoided reference to that which made each night a somber horror to them both. They had come out to get away for a short time at least from even thinking of it; and had chosen a path beside which the sea-tide's self rushed by, driving backward the river's sweeter waters!

And as if that were not enough – as if fate were determined that they should by no chance, nor for the briefest interval forget – out of a by-way that joined the Drive came a man, and he was leading a white horse.

7.

White Horses (Continued)

Vanaman's nerves were overtaut from strain and lack of sleep. He halted, with a muttered ejaculation.

'What is it?' asked the woman.

The surprise in her tone reminded him that Miss Robinson had not his reason for starting at the bare sight of a white horse. Her attention in reading of Lutz's death had been given to the fact of his suicide, almost ignoring the apparently irrational purchase of the horse, Mirror.

'Nothing,' the doctor replied to her query, and again they walked on.

The man and the horse were coming toward them, and now Vanaman himself wondered that the sight of the pair should have so shocked him. Save for the fact that the horse was white and the man a man, they had hardly a characteristic between them reminiscent of the Atlantic City episode.

Mirror had been a blooded animal, and so strikingly beautiful that even in the earlier newspaper account, before the reporter had learned the beast's pedigree, mention had been made of its appearance. This poor brute, on the other hand, might have been handsome a score of years ago; it was merely pitiful now. Gaunt, dirty, harness and collar-galled, its white hide yellow in great patches from lack of grooming, it limped along on swollen hocks like a very effigy of neglected, equine old age.

And save that he was not old, its human escort seemed in hardly better case. The purchaser of Mirror, though mud-splashed, had been noticeably well-dressed. This fellow was clad in a dirty brown shirt and disreputably ancient trousers; his feet were bare, and his untrimmed tow-colored hair stood out from his hatless head in absurd ragged points, among which clung bits of straw, as if the man had last slept in a stable.

From his gaunt face, tanned brown by wind and sun, pale gray eyes stared bleakly with an oddly vacant look, almost like the eyes of a blind man. That he was not blind, however, was presently proved, for meeting the two who had come out to forget, his bleak eyes shifted suddenly from vacancy to Leilah's face, from her to the doctor and back again. Then his thin-lipped mouth widened in a sneering grin.

Vanaman was in no mood to tolerate even silent insolence of that sort; his fists clenched, and in passing he half turned. The fellow was looking over his shoulder, still grinning. He jerked a dirty thumb backward, indicating the horse.

'Best I could get, matey,' he leered. 'Good enough, yer think?'

'What's that?' demanded the doctor.

'That's a horse,' the man explained, deliberately misunderstanding the question. 'A white horse. Don't blame yer for not bein' sure what it is, but what can yer expect for five dollars? I give all I had in the world fer it.' He laughed mirthlessly. 'That's more than Lutz give fer his, the tight-fisted rascal! Did yer read in the paper how he beat the price down from thirty-five hundred to three thousand? One like him would be bound to make that sort of break and lose out. Now I hold that havin' give my last cent fer this charmin' brute, my five-dollar plug is worth more than Lutz's three-thousand-dollar thoroughbred. What yer got to say to that, Dr Vanaman?'

The doctor eyed the man rather wildly. Just at that minute he was swept by a ghastly doubt that any of this was real; that he was not himself mad and subject to delusions of phantom sea-tides, hawk-faced old tyrants, amazing strangers, and white horses. Then he looked at Leilah, and recaptured his mental balance. He had not been alone in hearing that astonishing speech, for bewilderment and dawning dread were in every line of the woman's delicate features.

He whirled on the stranger almost fiercely.

'Who are you?' he snapped. 'How did you know my name?'

The vagabond's sneering grin widened.

'Why, d'ye see,' he drawled, 'I got reasons of my own fer keepin' track of what goes on in a certain house. That's how I knows yer name, matey. And I tells yer frank what you've likely guessed already ye'r mixed in a bad business, matey, and before ye'r done you'll be buyin' a white horse of yer own, or I miss my guess. And take my advice, matey. When yer buys it, don't yer make Lutz's mistake and think yer can wriggle out easy. Pay all you've got in the world, matey, down to the shirt on yer back. And yer can tell old millionaire Robinson that broke as I am, I wouldn't stand in his shoes fer three times all his money! Tell him Blair said that, will yer? Jim Blair. He'll understand. So-long, matey, me and beauty here's got a engagement.'

He jerked at the frayed rope which, in lieu of halter, was tied about the ungainly beast's neck, and lifting its drooped caricature of a head an inch or so it shambled on in the wake of its master.

Vanaman made no effort to follow or stop them. When a minute later he saw the pair turn off the drive, go plunging and stumbling down the embankment, and head for a reed-grown spit of land which extended a short distance into the river, he turned abruptly and caught Leilah's arm.

'Come away, Miss Robinson,' he said between his teeth. 'I have no right to interfere, and I'm not sure I wish to. But there's no need for watching them. Something is about to happen out there which would distress you. Come away!'

'But, doctor, that must be the very man you wished to trace – the one who sold Mr Lutz the green box! I remember Frisby said that he was tall and lean, very ragged and dirty, with pale eyes –'

'Come away!'

Almost forcibly, Vanaman drew her with him, and in half-frightened perplexity the woman yielded. Walking fast, they had soon reached the boulevard again, and were out of sight of the river. But though the woman, alarmed by his insistence, had not looked back, Vanaman had done so while they were still on the Drive – and had seen what he expected to see.

They had been out scarcely half an hour, and old Robinson looked up in angered surprise when, without any formality of knocking, the door of his study was flung open and Dr Vanaman entered alone. Then something he saw in the doctor's face and manner caused the old man's hawk-brows to draw more fiercely together.

'What has happened?' he snarled, 'Where's Leilah? Ye damned pup, if ye've let any harm come to my gal –'

'Your niece is perfectly safe, Mr Robinson.' For all the tension his eyes expressed, the doctor's voice was very cold and even. 'I wish and in fact I demand a little interview with you alone, Sir, and for that reason Miss Robinson has very kindly excused us both for a time. There are several questions to which I demand answers.

'Why did Jacob Lutz commit suicide when the white horse he had purchased escaped from his knife on Atlantic City beach?

'And why did that Jim Blair – yes, I thought you'd know that name! – why, I say, did Jim Blair, having also purchased a white horse, lead it to the river when the water was salt with the incoming tide and cut its throat? Why did he cut his throat there, so that the blood ran into the river? Come, Sir, you've been using me blindfolded long enough! If I'm to go any further in this cursed business, I've got to know where I'm going. Why were those things done?'

8.

Psychometry

To demand is very well, and not difficult for any one who is young, forceful, and keyed almost to breaking point by circumstances which in the normal course of a normal person's life have no right to be. To endorse those demands may or may not be quite so easy. In Mr Jesse J. Robinson, for instance, the demander of anything whatever, reasonable or otherwise, was likely to find a resistance more than proportionate to the force in action against it.

Dr Vanaman was young, strong-willed, and resolute. But at the end of that interview he knew that he had merely dashed himself against the steel of a will not only the full equal of his own strength, but having the advantage of a ruthless cunning to which he could by no means lay claim.

He had fancied that his feeling for Leilah, a secret almost from his own soul, was unsuspected by her uncle. Now he learned differently. Keen hawk-eyes had seen much more than they appeared to, and, at this first real rebellion of the slave he had taken unto himself, old Robinson tightened his grip in a very disconcerting manner.

'So ye won't stay by me without I satisfy your prying curiosity, eh? Ye'll leave me to fight my own battles this very night, without I account for the foolishness of them two durn fools, Blair and Lutz, and tell ye, besides, all I know about this here?'

His grasping claws caressed the green box, and his voice rose in snarling triumph. 'All right! Clear out, then, ye wuthless, quittin' whelp! Leilah and me, we can git on without ye! Leilah's a Robinson and the Old Nick himself, hoofs, horns, tail, and brimstone, can't make a quitter of that gal!

'Skeered, maybe; yes. But she'll stick by her old Uncle Jesse till Tophet freezes. You're sweet on that gal. Oh, yes, ye are, now; d'ye think old Jesse Robinson's a fool to believe ye've took a job that drags ye through hell every night, and kep' it even this long for any other reason?

'Well, then! Ye want Leilah should hev your job o' watching by me? I warn ye, that's what'll happen if ye quit. I can trust Leilah, and I've learnt I can trust you; but 'fore the Lord, there ain't another body living I'd want to take chances on trusting to watch by me right now! One of ye two I will have beside me. Which is it to be? You or – Leilah?'

'I'll stay,' conceded Vanaman rather hoarsely.

'Course ye will,' sneered the other, and added with one of his steely, flashing glances: 'That don't mean ye'll git Leilah, neither, mind. I aim to hev that gal marry somebody wuth while!'

The doctor set his teeth and fairly ground his temper under his heel. There was small point to be gained by giving rein to it. He had his choice: to hand over the full burden of those dreadful nights to the woman of the moonlight hair; or himself to carry on, and bear as best might be the gross insults which went with the singular service. He realized that Robinson was speaking again.

'Now we've got that all settled, I'll tell ye something, doctor. It's for your own good I ain't making the full truth known to ye. Blair knows it. Lutz knew part of it. I know as much as Blair. We three, I'm free to admit, hev all had some cause to worry. But Blair and Lutz and me, we've been in this thing a way that you nor Leilah ain't, and as long as ye jest obey orders and keep from pryin' too deep and don't git skeered of what can't really hurt ye, you're safe as a church and ye won't be buyin' any white horses, neither.

'Not but what white horses are good enough in a way. I named them two as fools, but I dunno but in Lutz's place or Blair's, I might try the same thing myself – mebbe. My own position's right different from theirs now, though. It ain't white horses he wants from me. He's like old Jesse Robinson; that's why I've got such a lot of respect for him and am kind of enjoying our little meet-up. His motto's the same as mine. What he wants he gets, and what he gets he keeps. All except this here box, and he's kinda lost his grip on this, eh? Well, then!'

'Mr Robinson,' broke in the doctor, rising suddenly. 'I do know why those white horses were bought, and I understand better than you think what it is you believe you're fighting. But whatever the history of the box – for whatever reason it is haunted by hallucination for those who own or are near it – the belief you hold is madness! Such things cannot be.

'Lutz went literally mad over the same delusion you cherish; you know how he ended. Blair is going the same road soon, or I mistook the look in his eyes to-day. For Heaven's sake, man, pull up before it's too late, and you and I and perhaps even that lovely young woman your niece – follow those other two! What you believe in is illusion – folly – outrageous superstition! But the real truth, whatever it is, has produced in that box an accursed thing. Get rid of it! Break it to pieces, or cast it into the sea if you prefer –'

He checked, amazed even yet by the really frightful anger which his tyrant's face was capable of expressing. The knotted brows writhed above eyes like points of blue fire; the beak-shaped nose seemed to curve more sharp and cruel, while out of that fanged, oblong aperture, his mouth, issued a sound that was not articulate, but the wordless savage warning of a predacious creature.

Before the torrent of objurgation he knew would follow could be uttered, Vanaman wheeled and left the study. He had failed, and must make the best of it, but he felt the need of getting a better grip on his own temper before taking any more of Robinson's uncalled-for abuse.

That night all up and down the Atlantic coast raged a storm such as even winter seldom looses, and from Nova Scotia to the Florida Keys the sea was flung, ravening upon the helpless land. The frail defenses of man went down before it, and in many a supposedly safe harbor, and in many a flooded coast town, the green hissing marauder claimed toll of human life.

Up the Delaware swept such a tide as she had not known in all her history, and the lower part of even Tremont, over fifty miles from the coast, was inundated by its far-flung rage. At Kensington, a few miles beyond, some of the great manufacturing plants were completely flooded. The Robinson Brothers' Engine Works suffered heavily, and next day the latter's amiable owner, after an early telephone call from the general manager at the plant, found occasion to express very forcible annoyance.

It was Sunday, but unlikely to be a day of rest for any one connected with the engine works. A large government contract stood in danger of being tied up, and Robinson, after a hurried breakfast, flung out of the house and into his car with the expressed determination to 'git that water drained off if I have to murder a few of them wuthless loafers who want to lay around and twiddle their thumbs and wait. Wait! Damn 'em! They'd wait till the cussed Delaware dries up, and me losin' money every day.'

He was gone, and a certain atmosphere of relief enfolded the house he had vacated.

For Leilah and Dr Vanaman, however, the relief was not so great as it might have been had they not been left to guard a blue-green, polished, beautiful enigma, the very sight of which they both loathed. Again its owner had extracted a solemn promise from his resentful but trustworthy slave not to let the box for one instant out of his sight and keeping.

'The cussed thing is mine,' he had emphasized. 'It's not Leilah's, and it ain't yours. Understand that, and –'

'If you have any mad idea that I want to claim ownership in it –' began the doctor indignantly, but Robinson had cut him short.

'Ye plaguey fool, no!' he snapped. 'Shet up and listen. This box is mine. You and Leilah, you're jest agents of mine, and though you're responsible to me ye ain't responsible to – to somebody that used to hev this box and is actin' up mighty dangerous trying to git it back. Don't ye ever dasst think of it as anybody's but mine; then I reckon you're safe enough. Fergit that warning and I won't guarantee nothing. Understand?'

'You know that I do not – not fully. But I shall remember what you said,' Vanaman told him.

After Robinson had gone the day passed quietly enough until midafternoon, when the door-bell rang and presently the butler brought Vanaman a card.

'Show the lady into the library, Frisby,' he instructed, after a moment's contemplation. 'And ask Miss Robinson if she will be so very good as to join me there at her convenience.'

He descended, taking the box with him, and when a few minutes later Leilah appeared in the library she found him conversing with a tall, angular, determined-looking woman dressed in black. Her iron-gray hair was fairly strained back under an old-fashioned black bonnet, and the stern severity of her countenance would have been rather appalling, had it not been relieved by a pair of very kindly, bright brown eyes, so like the doctor's own that Leilah instantly and correctly surmised blood relationship.

'Miss Robinson, I would like you to know my aunt, Miss Fellowes. This, Aunt Jane, is the young lady who, as I wrote you, shares with me the desire to see a very curious problem solved.'

'And as soon as I had Jack's letter I came straight on,' announced the visitor, in tones as positive as her appearance.

'That was extremely kind of you, and I am very pleased to make the acquaintance of a relative of Dr Vanaman.'

Leilah spoke cordially, though inwardly bewildered. Was this the 'person in New York' to whom he had referred as necessary to the second plan, which he would have preferred not to take? If so, what was that plan, and why had he hesitated over it? But as the conversation proceeded, her naturally quick intuition divined the reason well enough, and in connection with any other matter than the green box she might have found it just a little bit amusing.

Dr Vanaman's aunt was a spiritualist, and not only that, but a spiritualist of the most pronounced and aggressive school.

That 'Jack,' who according to his aunt had been a grossly blind materialist from his youth up, should have had to admit that there really was something in the world a bit past his understanding, seemed to give her something very like gloating triumph. Moreover, she had apparently assumed that from this on he was full convert to her own rather extreme views. 'Spirits,' 'communicators,' 'guides,' 'percipients,' and 'psychic forces' haunted that library in verbal form till in desperation the doctor held up a protesting hand.

'Aunt Jane,' he pleaded, 'I can't possibly swallow all that at once. Please don't be annoyed with me, but I really can't! Maybe everything you say is true. Maybe every inch of the space we move through is crowded with spirits, and maybe it's as easy to establish communication with Julius Caesar as it is to call up the telephone operator. But all that was not exactly what I wanted your help about. I'll admit that I have a strong natural aversion for belief in the supernatural. I believe that if apparently supernormal phenomena exist their cause can – must be traced to some natural law, not previously recognized, perhaps, but as fixed and actually natural as the law of gravitation.

'Now I know, Aunt Jane, that you've had some rather curious experiences of your own. You told me about them last year, and if I seemed to take them lightly may God forgive me, for what I have been through the last few nights. But never mind that now. You told me that you had seen some sort of visions, and heard voices –'

'I talked with your grandfather's ghost,' interpolated his aunt with abrupt firmness.

'Very well. You talked with grandfather's ghost. According to that, Aunt Jane, you must be what spiritualists term "sensitive." Now, with all due respect and apologies, I haven't sufficient faith in the veracity of a professional medium to trust one of them with a certain experiment I want made. In the case of this box' – he eyed the green thing that lay across his knees, and shuddered slightly, '– in the case of this box any one who is even slightly "sensitive" in the sense we mean should be able to prove or disprove my theory.'

'What is it about the box that has troubled you so much, Jack?'

His aunt's voice was suddenly as kindly and sympathetic as it had formerly been didactic.

'I would rather not tell you just yet. Miss Robinson and I wish to find out something about its history. I've heard that a medium can sometimes – er – tell the history of an object merely by touching it –'

'But I don't at all pretend to be a medium, Jack.'

'Miss Fellowes,' interposed Leilah, 'won't you please at least try to help us out? If you knew – if you could by any possibility guess the frightful – frightful horrors –'

Her voice trembled and she broke off, biting her lips. Miss Fellowes looked surprised; the sympathy in her brown eyes deepened.

'Why, you poor children! I had no idea there was anything very dreadful attached to the affair. Certainly, I'll do all I can to help. But you mustn't give way to fear, child. There is nothing in the spirit world to harm you. Sometimes people are harmed, but they are injured by their own fright, not by any evil influence. I myself have learned to fear nothing. I think I can truthfully say, Miss Robinson, that there is nothing in this world or the other of which I am afraid!'

She looked it, too, sitting bolt upright, shoulders back, sternly severe save for the betraying kindliness in her bright brown eyes. Somehow for all her talk of spirits there was a matter-of-fact practicality about Miss Jane Fellowes which made her very presence reassuring.

'Exactly what did you wish me to do, Jack? Of course, you mustn't expect me to go into a trance. As I said before, I don't even pretend to be a real psychic.'

'Well, you might take the box in your hands to begin with. And then if you – er – see anything, you can describe it to us.'

Despite recent experiences, Vanaman was feeling rather foolish over the affair. He wished the idea of asking his aunt to come on had never occurred to him. Very methodically she was removing her black silk gloves, rolling them up and placing them in her hand-bag. Her hands, Leilah observed, were beautiful; not the kind of hands one expected from those stern, almost harsh features. Long, slender, delicate, there was temperament in every line of them.

'I'll take it now, Jack.'

Fascinated, Leilah watched as the doctor half reluctantly placed his detested charge in the hands extended to receive it. What would come of this? Was there any chance that they were about to learn the dread secret which made that clouded, emerald-like thing a menace to sanity, at least, if dangerous in no worse way?

'It is extremely pretty,' commented Miss Fellowes' positive tones. She was turning it about, admiring the shifting shades of green. 'Oh! You were holding it upside down, weren't you? What is this red writing on the cover?'

'I don't know. Give the thing back to me, Aunt Jane. I was foolish to expect results from such an experiment and I don't like to see you holding it!'

'Why, Jack, you are really afraid of this box, aren't you? My dear boy, there is nothing in psychic experiences to harm one. If this beautiful little casket is haunted by the restless spirit of some past owner, we, I am entirely sure, have nothing to fear. Such apparitions, Jack, are caused by the effort of earth-bound souls to make themselves seen and known again in the material world. Spirits of that order are to be pitied, not feared.'

'Aunt Jane, I tell you this is not a matter of ghost-walking. The apparition that haunts the box – is not – human.'

'No? Really, you arouse my curiosity immensely. Perhaps one of the elementals has been playing tricks on you. Raja Ramput, one of our greatest teachers, told me with his own lips that he had seen a fire elemental – the spiritual essence of fire, you understand – play all about the room where a seance was going on, and apparently set the curtains in a blaze. But no real harm was done. The elementals are mischievous and like to frighten people when they can. I know better than to be afraid, however. Now I shall close my eyes, endeavor to make my mind quite blank, and if any definite ideas or visions come to me I'll let you know.'

Sitting up very straight and rigid, holding the box in her lap with long, delicate fingers resting lightly just over the scarlet inscription, she did close her eyes. Several minutes of dead silence ensued. Miss Fellowes was quiet as a graven image, and looked rather like one, too.

It occurred to Vanaman that any fearful qualities the box possessed might well be held in stern repression so long as it remained in the keeping of his Aunt Jane.

Then Leilah gave a low cry, and the doctor half started from his chair. There was reason for dismay.

Over those stern, determined features had swept a sudden and dreadful change. Every drop of blood seemed to leave the face in a moment, the very lips went blue-white, and the eyes flashed open with a look of such awful fear in their depths as Vanaman had never seen in the eyes of a living creature.

'Oh – how – horrible!' The voice was a rasping cry, harsh and unfamiliar. 'How horrible! The cities – the scarlet cities crashing – falling. Save me! Oh, God, won't anybody save me? There he is! There! It is he, I tell you! The archangel. Oh, God – it is the archangel. The archangel of the abyss –'

Leaping forward, the doctor snatched the green casket from his aunt's hands and fairly flung it upon the table. Then he caught her in his arms just in time to prevent her toppling sidewise to the floor.

Jane Fellowes who had been so sternly sure of her courage to face any abnormal phenomena, and 'feared nothing in this world or the other,' had fainted dead away from sheer terror.

9.
A Daring Challenge

And again Leilah and Dr Vanaman were alone with a problem not only unsolved, but which seemed even a shade more sinister for its startling effect upon a person of Miss Fellowes' previously fearless and determined character.

Under hastily applied restoratives she had soon recovered consciousness and seemed physically little the worse for her experience. But whatever strange vision had flashed before her closed eyes, she was either unable to recall it clearly, or literally dared not describe it. Recalling his own and Leilah's hesitation to express in words the cause for their worst fears, Vanaman rather fancied that the latter reason for her reticence might be the true one.

He had no heart to question his aunt very searchingly. She was tremulous and shaken as by some severe shock, and he felt sick with self-reproach that he had deliberately dragged another innocent victim within the green casket's evil influence.

Leilah, though with secret misgivings on her uncle's account, had urged Miss Fellowes to remain with them till the following day; but Dr Vanaman's aunt had had enough and more than enough of that house. A few short minutes, it seemed, had robbed her of all pretense to courage, and the mere vicinity of the green box appeared to cause her the most acute distress.

Vaguely she assured her nephew that she had been through an experience which cured her forever of any liking for or interest in the occult, entreated him to leave the house with her and promise never to return; and when he refused, insisted on at once taking her own departure.

Since Vanaman's solemn promise forbade him to desert his charge, Leilah ordered out the runabout and herself saw the poor woman to the railroad station and off on the first New York train.

Returning, she found the doctor still in the library, very meditative and depressed, though he greeted Leilah with attempted lightness.

'Archangels and scarlet cities are a new development,' he smiled.

'Not altogether so,' she corrected him.

'No? Have you seen –'

'Nothing that you have not. But I think you have forgotten or perhaps overlooked something. Wait.'

She rang for Frisby, and when the man appeared asked him to bring them the noon edition of yesterday's Inquirer. From somewhere at the back of the house he resurrected it, and alone once more the woman pointed to a sentence in the earlier account of Lutz's death.

'The man, who was well dressed but hatless, splashed with mud, and, according to Dolan, rather wild-eyed, made a muttered reply in which the guards could distinguish only some reference to an "archangel," and passed on.'

'You see?' commented Leilah quietly.

'I see nothing,' Vanaman protested, rumpling his reddish-brown hair till it stood up wildly. 'Archangels – scarlet cities – they only confuse what few coherent thoughts I had of the affair. Lutz muttered something about an archangel. But why should he sacrifice a white horse to an archangel?'

Leilah's eyes opened wide.

'You mean those two men bought white horses to sacrifice them?'

Vanaman nodded miserably.

'They most surely did. In all the ancient worship of the sea, whether under the older Greek name of Poseidon, or as the Roman Neptune, black bulls and white horses were considered the most acceptable offering. I had a very definite suspicion of Lutz's purpose when I first read that account. He didn't use his knife to strike at the lifeguard, as it says. He struck at the horse, but not Dolan. He meant to cut Mirror's throat there on the beach, and failing in that seems to have gone clean raving mad and drowned himself.

'When we met Blair at the river he was bound on a similar errand. I didn't interfere, because I was afraid of precipitating a similar result. He succeeded in making his offering, and may God let it bring him peace! Though it's a rankly pagan custom, I am beginning to understand how they may have been driven to it. But Poseidon, god of the sea, was not an archangel. Where does the archangel come in?'

Leilah did not reply, and he saw that she was staring with strange, fascinated eyes fixed on lucent depths of green. He snatched the box from the table, tucked it under his arm, and rose.

'You, at least, need not be sacrificed, Miss Robinson! If I swear to you that under no circumstances and for no reason, imaginable or otherwise, will I desert your uncle so long as he keeps this box – won't you in turn consent to leave here for a while? You have other relatives with whom you could stay. Go to them! I beg and entreat of you, go!'

The woman shook her head, smiling. This was not the first time Vanaman had voiced that plea, but his 'sprite of the moonlights' as he had fancifully thought of her, possessed a resolution firm as her uncle's, though of different quality.

'I couldn't possibly leave him,' she countered. 'He relies on me in many ways, and needs me now, I think, more than ever. I can't go, but you can. There is no claim of duty to hold you here, Dr Vanaman.'

He turned away, head slightly bowed. Sometimes the best and most innocent of women will administer a stabbing hurt and remain quite unconscious of causing it.

'I prefer to stay,' he said in a low voice, and carrying the box to the suite of rooms he shared with his employer, spent the rest of the afternoon alone with it.

Robinson returned late, tired out, and in an uncommonly savage humor. His mood found its appropriate victim in the man he held by a tenuous but unbreakable bond. Ruthless judge and manager of men that he had always been, the old hawk was sure of Vanaman as of Leilah, and since in his own peculiar way he really loved the latter and cared nothing about the former, the woman was peremptorily dismissed from her uncle's presence and Vanaman received full benefit of the evil temper generated by conditions at the engine works.

It was an unpleasant martyrdom, and before the evening was over the doctor hated Robinson as he had never known he could hate a human being.

Though the day had been fair, night promised another storm. Toward morning the promise was fulfilled with a violence that seemed to shake the very earth: and lying awake, expectant, Vanaman found it hard to quell and banish certain foolish notions.

Yet this night was better in one respect than any he had spent here. Brief snatches of sleep visited him, and from each he would start quiveringly alert; but not even once did the menacing hiss of a phantom but terrible approach mingle with the sounds of rain, raving against the windows.

Indeed, had Vanaman been willing to accept the belief he suspected Robinson of holding, he might have thought the inhuman thing which claimed the green box was using its utmost force in other ways, and had none to spare for empty hallucinations. As it was, grim pictures flashed before his fancy.

While the house shook in the grip of the unseasonable storm, he saw with the mind's eye an unconquered, ravening blackness, that gleamed translucent green when the lightning's lance shook above it. Over the globe's broad curve it roared hungrily, and the crests of its monstrous billows were tossed toward the clouds, like the myriad, wind-torn manes of white horses racing.

They flung themselves on the land, and the land vanished beneath their thunderous hoofs. A wailing rose in the night; earth shook and shuddered; mountains crashed into mighty flares of flame, and by the leaping light of those awful torches he saw the shrieking race of men devoured, swept away, made nothing. He saw earth open yawning mouths that swallowed whole cities, gulped and closed again. And where the cities had been – the ten glittering, scarlet cities – there surged and thundered the white-maned hosts of him.

Vanaman shook himself awake again and scowled vengefully across the room at a green box clutched tight in two claw-like hands. Better to lie awake than dream dreams like that.

Day returned at last, and again the lash of the tempest rested, and from north to south, down the long sweep of the Atlantic coast, men cursed, wept, counted their lost, and wondered.

Old Jesse J. Robinson had slept like a child, but the slightly better humor in which he awoke was quickly shattered by the morning's news. Grim-faced, steely eyes narrowed, he read of the ravages wrought by the sea while he slumbered.

Watching him across the breakfast table, Vanaman thought that so might appear the grim old tyrant of a city, reading the despatches that told of some strong enemy's gains. Of a beleaguered, beautiful, scarlet city that would not yield.

The doctor gave himself a mental shake. For Heaven's sake, what was coming over him? Continually, like a moving succession of small, bright pictures, the strangest ideas and fancies marched across the dull background of an over weary brain. He dared not even inspect them too closely. He remembered Lutz and Blair. Was that fate on its way to him? Then he glanced at Leilah, and steadied himself with an effort. His part was to guard her at any cost.

Robinson left shortly for his beloved and engine works; or so Vanaman supposed.

The old hawk's errand this time, however, proved to have been quite another than that of yesterday. The doctor had believed himself hardened to amazement and more or less proof against shocks; but the announcement made by Robinson on return, some hours later, strained his command to the uttermost.

On coming in, the old man greeted Leilah with a somewhat preoccupied air, then beckoned Vanaman.

'Want to talk with ye alone, doctor,' he said briefly, and led the way to his study.

He seated himself, motioning the doctor do likewise.

'Now,' he began, 'I want to ask ye a very important question. I want ye to think twice, and look yourself mighty close in the eyes before ye answer it. Are you game?

'Are ye a clean and honest-to-goodness, can't-be-made-a-quitter-by-nothin', a sure, dead game?'

Vanaman looked rather bored, and his eyes narrowed slightly.

'I really couldn't say,' he drawled. 'You will have to judge that for yourself, Mr Robinson.'

A reluctant grin twitched for an instant at the old man's mouth.

'Judging by short experience I've had with ye, I should say ye are. But if ye've got the least suspicion that, plug down deep enough, a body might find even the faintest shade of yaller, then take old Jesse Robinson's advice and clear out now, while ye've got the chance. For I'll tell ye something, son: Ye think ye've been pretty hardly used and badly tried; and so ye hev. But if ye stick now, I warn ye a trial's on its way to ye beside which what's passed was child's play! Understand?'

The doctor scowled.

'If you would have the commonplace decency, Mr Robinson, to be frank with a man who, you admit, has done his utmost blindfolded, that man might possibly not only understand, but be of far greater value to you.'

'So? But that's another thing for me to jedge, and I jedge differently. You suspicion what we're up against, but in the fool pride of your schooling and book knowledge ye refuse to believe in it. That's all right. You ain't old Jesse Robinson, and if ye did know the truth and believed it, I reckon ye'd hunt the nearest hole to hide in and be no more good to me. But this much I'll tell ye, and ye can make what ye like of it:

'What I want I get, and what I get I keep. That's been my motto always, and I intend to hold by it. But on the other hand, I ain't anyways as mean as some folks hold me. I ain't aiming to see whole cityfuls of people routed in this business. The fight's between me and him, and I'm willing to let it be so. What he gets he keeps; and what I get I keep.

'If he can take this here box from me fair, all right. But I don't jest reckon he can, and that's why he's raising murder over it trying to skeer me into giving up. To test that – fair – without involving any more of the general damage to property and life he's saw fit to work, I've done a thing that may or may not skeer ye, jest accordin' to how much of the truth ye believe and how near ye come to being dead up-and-down game – like me and Leilah.'

The old man's face had lighted with a grim, unholy daring, and his steely eyes glittered as they roved about the room. They came at last to fixed rest on the casket.

'We're going to sea, my son,' he announced abruptly. 'Me and this here green beauty and you, if ye've got the nerve, we're going to meet the party that wants my property, fair and open. There ain't nobody nor nothing can bluff nor bully old Jesse Robinson. I aim to prove that. They's a first-rate bit of sea-goin' shipping down at the docks. Her name's the Nagaina, and she was built for rough work up north. I'm told the storm ain't yet blowed that can down the Nagaina, so I reckon she's my boat. Leastways, I'm chartering her for a two month's cruise, and I aim to go aboard her this very day. Now, young man, are you game? Because if ye ain't, Leilah is, and I'll take the gal instead!'

10.

Outward Bound

Of actual facts transpiring through the remainder of that day, Dr Vanaman had afterward only a confused and indefinite memory. Perhaps lack of sleep had told on him more heavily than it would have done under normal conditions. Or perhaps his fear of the morning had not been wholly unfounded, and that which drove two such commonplace individuals as Blair and Lutz to offer up pagan sacrifice was beginning to set its deadly seal on him also.

Certain it is that all through the long afternoon, busy enough for others, but dreamily idle for the green casket's faithful guardsman, he was scarcely aware nor thinking of what went on about him, and dared he but close his eyes for an instant strange, fleeting visions flashed up behind the lids.

He had made his choice, where for him there was no choice. Let the truth be what it might, the mad voyage Robinson proposed would bring about the very thing Vanaman had urged in vain. Leilah would not desert her uncle, but the latter was leaving her, and on those terms Vanaman was ready if not exactly eager to accompany the green box and its owner to the devil, if need be.

Though he followed so little of what went on, that was a lively and exciting afternoon for many people. When Robinson chose to have things done in a hurry, as a rule they were done, for the old hawk's executive ability and knack of extracting from people efforts which surprised themselves, but not him, were marked as his stubbornness and indifference to the will or pleasure of any one but Jesse J. Robinson.

The Nagaina, fortunately for his sudden resolve, was already coaled, fully manned, and partly provisioned. She was a small but sturdy steamer, designed to fight through the perilous, ice-infested seas of the extreme north. Formerly used for the transportation of freight and passengers in the waters of northern Canada, she had been chartered from that service by an ambitious and wealthy young man, who had outfitted for an expedition.

The young man's sudden demise in a railroad accident had left the Nagaina's charter a useless asset of his estate, and the trustees had been delighted to receive Robinson's unexpected offer. The terms on which he relieved them of their white elephant included a haste in transfer that rather took their breath away; but the old millionaire had done an eccentric thing or so before in his life, and knew how to put this one through.

His own lawyers, well trained to execute any sort of sudden and complicated commands, met the trustees and wrestled with them. The will had not gone to probate, but a more or less legal loophole was discovered by which the trustees might act in this emergency. They found themselves shoved through it, a line of reasoning to use with the probate judge bestowed gratuitously upon them, the charter transferred, and Robinson's certified check in their hands, almost before it occurred to them that they might demand an extra bonus for such unseemly speed.

Almost, not quite. Robinson paid heavily for this particular eccentricity, but as they knew he could afford it his lawyers were not worried over that. Triumphant, they flung themselves into a taxi, motored straight to their employer's residence, and there spent a somewhat longer time in receiving his very precise instructions as to the handling of affairs in his absence, and particularly in case of his non-return. They may have wondered deeply as the rest of the world over the freak that was sending Robinson on so sudden a 'pleasure voyage' – he termed it that – and on such a vessel as the Nagaina. But if so, they kept their wonder to themselves. Had they not been wise enough to refrain from superfluous questioning, they would not have been attorneys to Jesse J. Robinson.

Down at the docks, meantime, a burly sea-captain swore, and still burlier stevedores sweated. The order to complete the Nagaina's provisioning and make her ready for immediate clearance had been received by Captain Porter with annoyance and dismay.

'A yacht!' he growled disgustedly to his second. 'They've made it a bloomin' yacht. We're to take a bloomin' millionaire on a pleasure voyage! It'll be, "Captain, put in at Bar Harbor," and "Captain, I've changed my mind, we'll make the Bahamas instead," and "Captain, spread an awning on quarter-deck; I want to take my bloomin' siesta there."

'I know 'em! I was second mate once on a Bermuda passenger boat, and there's no pleasin' 'em. I'm going ashore to buy some pink and blue ribbon, Mr Crosby, and when I come back you can tie it around her funnels before our new charterer thinks to order it done. Maybe that'll please him. Hell!'

To all of which Crosby listened with a wide grin, not sharing the bitter sentiments of his superior. A pleasure voyage, even with the most exacting of millionaires aboard, appealed to him as preferable to the rough hardships of the frozen north.

At six o'clock Captain Porter's anticipated trials began. A boat put off from the city wharf bringing a man who introduced himself as Robinson's valet, who demanded to be shown the cabin his master would occupy, and proceeded to rearrange and embellish it in a manner which completed Porter's disgust, and filled the steward, who helped, with amazed awe. The fellow had brought off a boat-load of 'silly, womanish junk,' as Porter characterized the soft mattresses, silken quilts, fine linen, and other luxuries with which the bare, dingy little stateroom presently incongruously blossomed. A complete Sevres dining service and silver appropriate thereto was the final straw. Porter clumped sadly up the companion ladder.

'Why didn't he charter a bloomin' yacht?' he mourned to his still grinning second. 'Why did he pick on me? Why didn't he charter a bloomin' yacht, all pretty mahogany and brasses? That's what I want to know!'

Nearly eight o'clock, and Robinson entered the room where Dr Vanaman brooded alone over his charge.

'We're leaving,' he said briefly. 'Are you ready?'

As the doctor made no reply, he approached, clutched his shoulder and shook him. 'What's ailing ye? Asleep?'

Vanaman stumbled to his feet.

'I'm tired,' he said heavily. 'But I'm ready to go.'

The millionaire cast him a sharp, almost troubled glance, but made no comment, and the two passed out to the car, waiting ready in the porte-cochere. As they went Vanaman was vaguely conscious of something wrong or missing in this departure. It was not the green box. He was carrying that in the leather handbag. His hat? No; that was on his head. And his personal luggage had been packed earlier and taken down with Robinson's things. What, then? He could not think, and for sheer weariness ceased trying.

The chauffeur was holding open the door of the closed car, and as Robinson pushed his companion ahead he stumbled clumsily in and almost fell into the rear seat.

'What is it, Dr Vanaman? Are you ill?'

That low, drawling sweet voice. Now he knew what had been wrong; whom he had missed. Leilah had not said good-bye to them, and no wonder! The old hawk had tricked him. He had never meant to leave the woman behind. For an instant, under stimulus of indignation, the stupor lifted, and he was all angry protest.

'You here, Miss Robinson! But you are not going with us! You're not! I – I forbid it –'

'That'll do, son,' snarled Robinson. He stepped in and took his seat; the chauffeur, who already had his directions, closed the door, and in another moment they were rolling down the Drive.

'Leilah wanted to come,' continued the old man composedly, 'and I don't just reckon it's for you to forbid or command my gal from doin' anything she and me choose for her to do. Understand?'

'I – guess so.'

Numb weariness was on him again, and it was pleasant to lean back in soft cushions, and feel the warm, delicately fragrant nearness of – of some woman he had once known, pitied, and adored. But that, of course, had all been a very long time ago.

'Fog!' snarled a voice. 'Cuss it, we'll have to lay in the river till she clears. Might just as well have stayed to home!' Again roused for a moment, Vanaman saw that the car windows were blanketed with thick white mist, through which the lights of shops and street lamps glowed in hazy, shifting change. They were in the lower part of the city now, and nearing the docks.

Presently the car had rolled through an open gateway and part way down the long reach of a public wharf. It came to a stand, and the chauffeur appeared at the door.

'Will you get out here, Sir?'

'How in time do I know?' snapped his employer. 'Ain't ye got any sense at all, Murphy? They's four or five stairways on this wharf. Walk along and find which one the Nagaina's launch is waiting at. I give orders,' he added as the man moved off on his mission, 'that the launch was to meet us here round 9 o'clock. It's 8:45 now, and she ought to be on hand – somewheres. Cuss the fog! Can't hardly see ten foot through it down here.'

Murphy returned and climbed back in the car.

'A little further along, Mr Robinson,' he informed over his shoulder, as they started.

A few seconds later and they had halted again. The tall, dim figure of a man loomed grayly beside the door. He opened it without waiting for the chauffeur.

'This is Mr Robinson? We are ready for you, Sir.'

The voice was low, deep, and well modulated, though the fog lent it a muffled and far-away sound.

'Help me out, can't ye?' came Robinson's eternal snarl. 'That's better. Durn ye, ain't ye got any sense to grab my arm that way? Ye durn near broke it!'

'I beg your pardon, Sir.'

The dim figure relaxed its overpowerful grip and stood back a pace or so. Leilah, who was nearest the door on this side, stepped lightly out and turned.

'Dr Vanaman! Uncle Jesse, I believe the doctor is ill! He hasn't moved nor spoken a word since we left the house.'

'Nonsense! Jest asleep again, I reckon. Hey, doctor, wake up!'

He leaned in and shook at Vanaman's knee.

'I'm coming.'

He had heard every word spoken, but because of the heavy drowsiness that was on him had preferred to sit quiet. Something was wanted of him now, it appeared. He managed to stumble out on the wharf and stand there stupidly quiescent.

'Where's that bag? Why, ye left it on the seat! Humph! Well, so long as you're too durn sleepy to know what you're about, I reckon I'll keep charge of it myself. That's all, Murphy. Take the car home and mind! Don't ye dasst use up my gasoline joy-riding round while I'm gone.'

'No, sir.'

Murphy had touched his cap and was slowly backing along the comparatively narrow wharf. The head-lamps cast funnel-shaped cones of light through the slowly drifting strata of river mist, and one of these cones rested for a long moment on the dim figure that had met the car. The head was bare, the face heavily bearded, and the man seemed to be wrapped in a long, gray cloak. Then his deep, muffled tones were speaking again:

'Will you come aboard now, sir? Everything has been prepared, and we are ready to sail with the outgoing tide.'

'Sail?' repeated Robinson. 'The Nagaina's a steamer, ain't she?'

'Oh, yes. The Nagaina is a steamer. But I have been long – very long – associated with sailing vessels, and the word comes easily to my lips. Pray, pardon it.'

'Humph! Officer, be ye?'

'I have the honor to be captain, sir.'

'Captain Porter, eh? Why didn't ye say so, straight off? Think ye can make it down-river in this dirty fog?'

'The fog will not interfere with our sailing, sir. If you will kindly accompany me down these steps, I will help you into the small boat that is waiting.'

'Well, then! Ye don't need to be so durn ceremonious over it,' grumbled Robinson. 'Doctor – consarn the fool! I believe he's asleep again! Hey, doctor, wake up!'

Vanaman straightened with a start, and this time actually roused enough to offer Leilah his assistance in descending the dozen wooden steps that led to a small floating platform at water-level. The small boat referred to was drawn up alongside. It was not the gasoline launch Robinson had expected, however, but an oar-propelled craft. Three oarsmen could be faintly discerned occupying its thwarts, and a fourth waited on the platform, holding a lantern.

Without at all thinking about it, Vanaman observed that the lantern was not the common ship's type, but of cubical shape with ornamental wrought-iron framework forming a lattice tracery over side panels that might have been made of old-fashioned horn, not glass, so dim and yellow was the light transmitted from within.

'If you take your seat on that forward thwart, sir –'

'Ladies first,' snapped Robinson fussily. 'Git in, Leilah.'

The tall captain made a sudden gesture, almost as though to prevent the woman from obeying. But Leilah was quick and deft in her motions, and already she had stepped in and taken the place indicated. The old hawk handed her the leather bag that contained his prey, and a moment later was seated beside his niece. When Vanaman would have followed, however, the captain caught his arm in that overpowerful grip of which Robinson had complained.

'I am sorry, sir,' he said firmly. 'The boat will not carry so many, Mr Robinson. When we have put yourself and the young lady aboard, there will be time enough to return for this gentleman. I understand you are in great haste to reach the sea. But so small a delay will matter little, and moreover, once started we shall sail very swiftly, for the tide will carry us along – the outflowing tide.'

'The outflowing tide,' gravely echoed the man with the lantern.

And as if in sentiment confirmation of the words, the dark

waters that raced gurgling and seething past the piers jerked strongly at the prow of the boat, so that it swung suddenly outward. The man with the lantern stepped aboard in haste and dropped to the fourth oarsman's seat. The tall captain gave Vanaman a push that sent him stumbling back against the steps, and himself made a flying leap across the half-dozen feet of racing water that already intervened between boat and platform.

He landed neatly, standing in the stern sheets. Vanaman, staggering up, had a momentary glimpse of him as a tall, gray figure, outlined vaguely against the dim lantern-glow and very wraithlike because of the fog that swirled between. The muffled but unmistakable cry of a frightened woman drifted back to him.

And then he was alone in the dark on a little platform, beneath which unseen water seethed and raced. The tide – the outflowing tide –

Like a riven veil, or as if with the passing of the green casket some evil charm had been lifted from his brain, the stupid daze which had for hours possessed Vanaman cleared and was gone.

'Leilah! Oh – Leilah!'

Springing to the platform edge, he shouted her name again and again. There returned to him no responding cry, but close at hand, just behind him, in fact, he heard a noise as of smothered laughter. Wheeling, he collided with the person who had found cause for mirth in his fear-stricken shouts. His hands closed on lean shoulders.

'Sheer off there, matey! I ain't huntin' trouble.'

'Blair!' gasped Vanaman. Though he had heard the man's voice only once before, that once had been under conditions to impress its tones on his memory. He dropped one hand, but slid the other down to the fellow's upper arm where he held him firmly.

'You, Blair!' he choked. 'In some cursed way or other you are behind all that's happened! What are you doing here? Why did the Nagaina's boat take those two and leave me? Answer, or – or, by heaven, I'll strangle an answer out of you!'

In the dark his free hand found the other's throat and closed on it convincingly. The man struggled, but with so feeble a resistance that even in his overwrought state Vanaman was suddenly ashamed, and his grasp relaxed.

At the same time, the put-put of a rapidly nearing motor throbbed through the fog. Mingled with it came the sound of an aggrieved and mournful voice.

'Shut her off, Mr Crosby. The bloomin' wharf's dead ahead. And now I suppose we can wait an hour or so till our millionaire charterer shows up. I know 'em! Always an hour or so behind time. But maybe it will please him that I came after him myself and then had to wait an hour.'

'Hell!'

An intolerable suspicion stirred in Vanaman. As the shape of the small launch materialized through the fog, red and green lamps a-glitter, he greeted it in a hoarse question.

'From the Nagaina?'

'My boat,' resignedly acquiesced the voice. 'Are you Mr Robinson? Or is there a Mr Robinson waiting up on the wharf? Because if there is, tell him his dunnage is all aboard, and Captain Porter has come ashore in person to do the proper honors and fandangos expected of a yacht captain. And that ought to please him,' he added sotto voce to his second, who was already scrambling out on the platform, lantern in hand.

But on Vanaman, the icy fingers of dismay had closed more tightly.

'For God's sake, get back there!'

He fairly thrust the Nagaina's astonished second officer back into the launch and himself followed, dragging Blair along.

'Mr Robinson and his niece have been stolen – kidnapped!' he announced between his teeth. 'Another boat was here – another man who called himself Captain Porter. I was purposely left behind, and those two taken. Get out on the river – quickly! Somewhere out there is either a small boat or a ship that means to go down-river with the tide!'

II.
James Blair, A. B.

Captain 'Tom' Porter, well known and liked among the blunt, outspoken fraternity of his own kind, had found cause for melancholy in the sudden change of charterers which made the sturdy old Nagaina a pleasure craft and demanded of himself the graces and, as he chose to take it, servility of a yacht-captain. Discovering, however, that scoundrels unknown had illicitly borrowed his identity and that of his ship and thereby wrested his despised charter from him, Captain Porter's viewpoint toward the latter abruptly changed. Had there been stolen from him some prized and long-treasured possession, the captain could have been no more personally outraged and indignant.

Jesse J. Robinson was his – his charterer! And the captain's ideas of property rights seemed well on a par with Robinson's own.

Mr Crosby suggested that before attempting to quarter the river on their own account, the harbor police be notified. The captain swore and ordered him to put back for the Nagaina instantly.

'We can wire the police, and wireless every ship and station down the river. Nobody but a criminal or a fool will be moving in this weather. It's safe to demand that any craft that is moving is to be held up. We don't know exactly what her bloomin' type is, but she wears sail and she's medium big one, by the cut of her bow and forerigging.'

'What's that?' cut in Vanaman. 'What do you know of her rigging? I saw nothing but the small boat.'

'And we saw that and more, too,' was Porter's unexpected retort. 'Matter of fact, we passed your bloomin' kidnappers just at the identical moment when they were hoisting their tender aboard. Mr Crosby there, not knowing any vessel was berthed near the Nagaina, all but fouled their bow in the fog. How they got to lay to so near without our knowing it is past me. There wasn't a bloomin' sign of a vessel anchored anywhere around the Nagaina when the fog shut down.

'First we knew of her, there was her dolphin figurehead right on top of us. I yelled, and Mr Crosby sheered off and just missed fouling her cable at that. It was hove up short, all ready for a quick getaway, as I know now. As we turned I saw the lines of her rigging sharp and black for just a minute against her riding lights. And I saw and heard them hoisting their tender in over the port bulwark. Then the fog shut in thick, and I didn't see any more, but if that wasn't your kidnappers, call me a Dutchman and be done.

'Of course, they have auxiliary power or they couldn't go down-river without a tug, fog or no fog. But she's a sailing-craft of some sort, painted black, with a red dolphin for her figurehead and a funny kind of swell-out and curve back cut to her stern that I never saw on any other boat. She'll be easy enough to identify, once caught.'

'How do you know this vessel you describe isn't still anchored where you saw her?'

'I bloomin' well know it! If she's there she's at the bottom, and we just now cruised by over her. Mr Crosby, I make the Nagaina a half-point up from this course.'

'Half-point it is, sir,' muttered his second, and the wheel-spokes shifted a trifle under his hands.

Vanaman realized that by instinct or knowledge almost uncanny to a landsman the captain was sure of his position on the fog-blanketed river as if the time had been high noon, with a clear sun shining.

'By the way,' continued Porter, 'who's the party you're clingin' to with so much affection? One of the kidnapper's gang?'

Vanaman glanced at the dilapidated figure which drooped dispirited and silent beside him.

'I think possibly he is, though I'm not certain. Tell you all about it later, captain. This is the Nagaina, isn't it?'

A black, wall-like expanse had loomed above them, and a minute later Vanaman was ascending the ladder with an agility lent him by the keenest anxiety. Blair followed without protest, and Captain Porter was no sooner on deck than he sent one of his men to rout out the wireless-operator and another for his chief engineer.

Before the fog drifted in on her, the Nagaina had been expected to clear that night. The pilot was aboard, and the fires were still banked under her boilers. The engineer promised steam within the half-hour, and the pilot, though not without considerable protest, finally consented to do his best toward conning the Nagaina downstream.

'Though if she rams her nose in a mud bank don't blame me,' he added gloomily. 'I'm no X-ray artist to keep the channel in this weather.'

'The bloomin' weather wasn't too thick for that other craft.'

'No, and she's very likely hung up on a bar this minute, waiting for your fool boat to ram in beside her.'

'I don't ask anything better,' retorted Porter, and there was a certain grim and anticipatory pleasure in his tone. The Nagaina's master was rather like the stout old steamer he commanded: a fighter born.

Till urgent messages had been sent to the Tremont harbor police and other stations both up and down the river, neither the captain nor Vanaman cared to take time for explanation on the latter's part. The bare facts of the abduction with what description they could give of the suspected vessel, were sufficient to set the forces of the law in motion. They also brought a police boat nosing through the fog in search of the Nagaina's berth, though by the time it arrived there the berth was empty and the Nagaina cautiously feeling her way down-channel.

By wireless, however, she remained in touch with the shore stations, and there was a bare chance that she might overhaul the black, dolphin-headed stranger even before the latter could be intercepted by the authorities. The hoarse hooting of her siren rang out belligerently. She snorted and puffed like a large, canary sea-beast, her propellers half the time in reverse as she fought against being carried along with too dangerous a speed by the racing current. She was clumsy and noisy, the Nagaina, but very honest and resolute.

The pilot had taken the bridge, and not being needed there Porter found time at last to question Vanaman more fully. With that mysteriously recrudescent individual, Jim Blair, still in tow, the doctor accompanied Porter into the privacy of the charthouse and there laid before him exactly as much as he deemed fit of events leading up to the abduction.

On the stranger side of the affair he touched not at all, merely stating that Mr Robinson had in his possession a certain casket, of contents unknown to him, Vanaman; that Mr Robinson had many times referred to some person or persons, also unknown, who wished to deprive him of the said possession; that Mr Robinson had the casket with him when abducted; and that the simplest assumption seemed to be that the abductors and the supposititious claimers of Mr Robinson's property were identical.

As he talked, it occurred to Vanaman that he was probably telling the truth.

Since the moment when he found himself left at the wharf, and his brain had cleared of that obsessing stupor, all the supernormal quality of the affair had seemed to grow steadily more questionable, fading to unreality like the uncertain memory of a dream – illusion – hallucination; three words that cover a multitude of otherwise inexplicable phenomena.

Certainly the abductors of Robinson and his niece had been no empty phantoms, but flesh-and-blood men. His arm still ached faintly where the tall captain had gripped it. The boat in which Leilah and her uncle were carried off – that was most assuredly a real boat. Captain Porter had seen the real ship to which it returned. And in good earnest, looking backward, old Robinson might from many of his remarks have been on guard against enemies far more human and credible than the vague, monstrous thing whose apparition haunted the green box.

In fact, what is generally termed 'natural common sense' informed the doctor very positively that while he and several other people had been to a certain extent victimized by singular illusion, to-night's event was – must be – of another order and belonging to the category of purely human and material activities.

Presently Mr Crosby appeared in the open doorway of the chart-house.

'Black craft with a red dolphin figurehead sighted at Bombay Hook little over an hour ago, sir,' he announced cheerfully. 'Reported by the tug Jersey Queen. We just now got in touch with her.'

'Bombay Hook? Over an hour ago?' repeated Porter sharply. 'The Jersey Queen's dreaming! Or else there are two red dolphins cruising ahead of us. Our boat can't have made Bombay Hook even yet, much less an hour ago. It's rank impossible.'

That lean wreck of a man, Jim Blair, seemed to rouse a trifle.

'Beg pardon, sir,' he interposed. 'If yer knew him yer wouldn't talk of nothing being impossible. That's his ship, sir, with the dolphin to her bow. And she's went down fast, of course, with the outflowing tide.'

Porter stared and the sailor stared back composedly; but there was a look in his pale, bleak eyes that after a moment made the captain glance toward Vanaman with a questioning lift of the brows, while his lips silently formed a word. The doctor shook his head.

'I'm not sure,' he murmured; then aloud: 'Blair, whom do you mean when you speak of "him"?'

The sailor's mouth widened in a sneering, almost foolish grin.

'If yer don't know already, Dr Vanaman, yer better off not to.'

'But I wish – I demand to know!' All the uncertainty, the

unnatural fears and the maddening doubts that had made the last few days an unremitting torment surged up as one great, urgent question. 'Blair,' he continued tensely, 'you are going to tell me every single thing you know about this cursed business, and you are going to tell it now – quick!'

'I ain't got any objection,' conceded the sailor, unexpectedly pliable. 'Fer a fact, I'd rather like to get it off my chest. But I warns yer fair, doctor, yer sittin' in a dangerous game if yer listens.'

'Tell the truth, my man,' put in Porter sternly. 'You admit that you know something of the gang who have made off with Mr Robinson and his niece. That admission alone is enough to jail you. Tell the full truth, and in return we'll do what we can to save you from the law.'

The sailor flung back to his head and laughed, a wild peal of merriment with an eldritch note in it that sent a shiver or so down Porter's back. 'Law!' Blair gasped presently. 'Law-man's law – to deal with him, and with me that's marked fer his! Wait! I knows yer don't mean to be funny. It's only that yer don't understand. I'll tell it all straight from the beginning, and whiles I talks yer can listen, and while yer listens we'll all go down the river with the outflowing tide – down the river to him!'

That story which Blair the sailor related standing in the yellow-lighted chart-room, hazy with fog, was a wild, long tale; too long and in many parts too incoherent for a verbatim report of it to be rendered here. Many times Porter, incredulous and increasingly suspicious of the fellow's sanity, would have cut him short; but Vanaman would not have that.

Porter had never sat and watched the sea-tide sweep in, frothing and impossible, miles away from the coast; had never seen phantom waters swirl and mass themselves and give birth to dark terror's self. No matter how mad and wild the tale in its texture might be, so must be the facts to explain a mystery fully as wild and mad.

The very beginning of the story, however, sounded sane enough. Early in the previous spring James Blair, A. B., had shipped at Liverpool in the old square-rigged merchant-vessel, Portsmouth Belle, bound with a mixed cargo for British Guiana. Two weeks out the ship encountered a dead calm with heavy, lowering weather, and a few hours later was swept toward the very clouds, as it seemed to Blair, on the crest of an enormous wave, which was in turn succeeded by two lesser ones.

'That's probably true enough,' commented Porter. 'Lisbon reported a moderate-sized tidal wave last May. Did some damage to shipping in waters north and east of the Azores, too.'

The Portsmouth Belle, continued Blair, survived the greater wave and its followers, and also laid to under storm staysails, outlived the tornadolike gale which ensued. When the wind somewhat lessened, its direction being N-N.E., the ship was allowed to run before it, and very soon thereafter was found to be scudding through a sea whose billows were curiously flattened and without foam or crests. The water, in fact, proved to be heavy with a grayish, ashlike substance, and being in the first mate's watch, Blair learned from him that the substance was indeed ash and cinders of volcanic origin.

The wind died still further, the sea became practically flat, and the Portsmouth Belle for a long time forced her way with great difficulty through this scum of ash, which by test was in many places found to be over a foot thick. The sky was continually overcast, the heat well-nigh unendurable, and a whisper went about the ship that the navigating officers were, to use Blair's phrase, 'going it blind,' due to some magnetic injury to the compasses. Spotting no other vessels, and being unsupplied with wireless, their exact position through these days was extremely uncertain.

May 17, when Blair understood they should have sighted the low peak of Corzo in the Azores, they were still surrounded by an unbroken horizon of sickly gray, the sea being dotted at one point, however, by a short, low bar of black which roved on closer approach to be a small island. Mr Kersarge, the first mate, informed Blair that this was in all probability new land, flung up by the submarine earthquake and eruption which had caused the tidal, or more properly speaking, the seismic wave.

Captain Jessamy elected to go ashore here, and Blair was one of the party of five seamen who accompanied him.

Rowing in that ash-encrusted sea was like propelling a boat through thick, half frozen slush, and the journey of, say, a half thousand yards required over an hour of strenuous exertion. They arrived at last, however, and Captain Jessamy was first to set foot on the strange bit of vapor-steaming rock extruded by the convulsive forces at work below.

Blair was the only one to follow him, and for an excellent reason. The other four seamen were all barefooted; but Blair, 'tipped off,' as he phrased it, by the mate, had brought along a pair of shore-boots. The rock was still hot enough to preclude any comfort in walking about, even for a man shod in heavy leather, and with naked feet the adventure became one of downright torture.

'And me,' said Blair, 'bringin' them boots along just to walk myself straight through the gates of hell! I wisht the old man had died before he ever seen that island! I wisht Mr Kersarge had died before he ever tipped me off to take them boots along! I wisht –'

'That will do, my man,' Porter cut in coldly. 'Cursing your officers will not finish this long-winded yarn you're spinning. Anyway, I fail to see how a volcanic island near the Azores can bear on the kidnapping of a bloomin' millionaire down the Delaware.'

'Yer will see, sir. But if yer don't want to hear it, I'll lay off.'

'Let him finish, Captain Porter – please,' intervened the doctor. 'Get ahead, Blair, and make it as short as you can to save time.'

'I will, sir, though it seems funny to talk of savin' time when yer tellin' of his doings. What's time to him? Why a matter of twenty thousand year or so ain't no more to him than five minutes is to you and me. Time! All right, sir; I'll get under way again.'

Near the center of the island, from which Captain Jessamy kept a safe distance, fearing poisonous vapors, were some masses of brilliantly scarlet rock, in form and juxtaposition vaguely suggesting the shapes of ruined buildings.

'Scarlet?' repeated the doctor.

'Red,' said the sailor. 'Red as new blood that's just been shed; red as the writin' that lays across what he's took again for his own; red as the ten red cities – ah, yer has seen a thing or two fer yer own self, doctor, ain't yer?'

'Never mind what I may have seen. Get on with your story.'

'Oh, I'm tellin' yer fast enough. It was while the old man – beg pardon, Captain Porter, sir; I mean Captain Jessamy – it was while he was peerin' at them old red walls through his binoculars that I first seen it. There was chunks and roundish balls of lava layin' all about in the wet ash. Black they was mostly, with dull red specks. This here was different. It was green – bright green, like grass almost; grass that blood has been sprinkled over in pretty little shiny red drops. And it were shaped real regular, almost like a box.

' "Captain Jessamy, sir," says I, "can I carry this here along when we goes? I could hollow it out to a box like, and maybe sell it ashore." And the old man, he laughs and says: "Sure. Help yerself to anything you find on this land, Blair. I reckon nobody won't come around claimin' no property yer removes from here."

'Just like that. He reckoned nobody would be wanting or claiming it from me. So I wraps it up in my shirt, because it's too hot to hold, and just like that I walks straight through the gates of hell, sirs.'

12.
Sea-God's Prize

*'What makes that ship drive on so fast.
What is the OCEAN doing?'*

THE RHYME OF THE ANCIENT MARINER

The sailor paused, bleak eyes pale and vacant almost as a blind man's. Again Mr Crosby had appeared in the doorway.

'Black vessel with a red dolphin reported from Henlopen, sir. One of the lighthouse men was out in the bay hauling his lobster-traps, just missed being run under.'

'Cape Henlopen! Worse and more of it. How long ago did your lobster-fishing lighthouse man have his bloomin' dream?'

'Nearly two hours, sir.'

'Fine!' Porter nodded sarcastic approval. 'Red dolphin made Bombay Hook in ten minutes, and Cape Henlopen three minutes later. Great old clipper. Mr Crosby, see to it, please, that our own lookouts stay awake. Our craft is somewhere on the river not far ahead, unless we've passed her.

'The fog has thinned a bit, sir. I'm nearly sure we haven't passed any craft near her tonnage in the channel.'

'Isn't it possible,' suggested Vanaman, 'that the ship we are after has anchored somewhere close to shore? The men might have deserted her and taken their prisoners to land.'

Porter's broad shoulders shrugged.

'Possible, of course. But if they meant to do that, why use a ship at all? No, I believe Friend Dolphin has figured on the fog to prevent pursuit or interference, and is making for open sea. Once outside she may have arranged a rendezvous with some other craft, intends to transship her prisoners, and sail off, innocent as you please, with no evidence aboard to convict her.

'That is, if they have any object such as ransom in keeping Mr Robinson prisoner. If they are only after this green box you talk of, they may carry him what they consider a safe distance up or down the coast and then put him and his niece ashore. We might be able to guess their intentions better if we knew a trifle more about 'em. Get ahead with that yarn you're spinning, Blair. And make the rest of it pretty bloomin' short and to the point.'

'I'll try, though there really ain't any hurry, sir. Yer might as well try to overhaul the Flyin' Dutchman as that craft with the red dolphin.'

Aboard the Portsmouth Belle again, Blair had stowed away the block of green lava and thought no more of it for a while. That night he dreamed of 'Belle Island,' as Captain Jessamy had named the risen bit of old sea-bottom; but the dream, though unusually vivid, he had laid to the restless slumber that had been induced by the heat.

Next day he occupied his leisure time in chiseling and rubbing down the block of lava, and finally induced the ship's carpenter to lend him a saw with which he proceeded to divide the comparatively soft material into two parts. Having sawed into it a bare quarter-inch a fragment of the lava broke away, disclosing what he at first took for a quartz-crystal nucleus in the block. Easily breaking away the remainder of the outer crust, he found, enclosed as in a cyst of the volcanic material, the green casket itself.

He was alone in the forecastle, and his first instinct was to conceal the find. To a man of Blair's limited education and mental attainments the extraordinary quality of his discovery appealed scarcely at all. To him, the disclosure of a probable relic of remote antiquity meant no more than if, walking along a city street, he had stumbled across a wrapped package, opened it, and found a jewel casket.

The interest was wholly in the casket's possible value to himself. Speculation as to its previous possessors was beside the mark; and his ignorance saw nothing miraculous in the object's perfect preservation through the volcanic heat which, rising to a possible two thousand or so degrees Centigrade, will melt the hardest rock and reduce metals to their gaseous form.

Failing to open the casket easily, and hearing one of his mates descending the forecastle ladder, he hastily concealed it in his bunk, complained to his fellow seaman that the lava block had crumbled to bits under the saw, and carrying the fragments on deck, flung them overboard. His chief concern at this time seems to have been lest Captain Jessamy learn of the casket's existence and take it from him.

Ere he could make further secret effort toward opening the box, a gale arose and the ship was soon discovered to be taking in water at an alarming rate. It was presumed that her seams had opened, due to the severe wrenching suffered in meeting the seismic wave and the tornado that succeeded it.

'They didn't know about him,' grinned Blair, vacant-eyed. 'And neither did I – yet. He was just waking up to notice that I'd stole what he meant to keep. He's kind of lazy and sleepy, I guess, sometimes. Like of them big snakes you'll see in the jungles south of Cancer. It'll feed full and then lay in the sun and doze and dream fer days, maybe, or maybe months. Just so, him. He was trying already to get back his own, but only half-trying. He'd lift up his big, lazy waves and slap at the old Portsmouth Belle. And she'd shiver and writhe and her seams would open a bit; kept all hands at the pumps in two-hour shifts till our hands was like red meat and our backs like to break. But he wasn't really awake yet, nor half-trying.'

'Dr Vanaman,' broke in Porter brusquely, 'is it worth while –'

'I wish to hear this story exactly as he is telling it.'

There was a quiet, dogged determination in the doctor's voice which again silenced Porter for a time. After all, till they ran down Red Dolphin, little could be done but wait. As well listen to Blair's wanderings as stand about idle.

The Portsmouth Belle, continued Blair, had long since passed beyond the ash-infested area. As in her leaky condition more danger would have been involved by the strain of lying-to than letting her run, the ship had been put before the wind, double reefed, and was driven along in a practically sinking condition till she encountered the Taconia, an oil-tanker bound in ballast for Tremont.

Salvage of the Portsmouth Belle was not attempted, but the Taconia's commander released the small quantity of petroleum oil which remained in the tanks, thereby so smoothing the rough waters in his immediate vicinity that it was possible to transship the old square-rigger's officers and crew to the tanker.

Thereafter the Taconia suffered a peculiarly stormy and difficult passage, but at length made port at Tremont, up the Delaware.

'He ain't so sure of himself, I reckon, in dealin' with steel ships, and steam, and oil like they turned loose on him to get us aboard the tanker. Or else, as I says before, he wasn't half-waked up yet. Anyways, we was landed safe at Tremont, like I says. The other fellers had began to fight shy o' me, though. Reckon I'd say a thing now and then they couldn't figger out the sense of. Captain Jessamy paid us all off square, like we'd made the full voyage we shipped fer. I will say them British lime-juicers treats yer white. The officer fellers all scattered, some shippin' again from Tremont, some drifting over to New York. But me, I stays where I landed, bein' more or less scared, and not quite knowin' what to do.'

'Why were you frightened?' queried Vanaman, though he knew the answer.

'Dreams,' said Blair. 'Just dreams. Sounds a triflin' matter to scare a knockabout feller like me that's sailed here and there pretty nigh all over the world, lived hard, and been treated rough. But there's dreams yer can forget, and others yer can't, and the kind that was comin' to me had a trick o' carryin' over into hours when I was awake.

'I seen things I dassn't tell of; and I've walked the streets of Tremont when the walls of the ten red cities seemed crashin' all about me. I've stood on the docks by the river and seen the river spread and stretch out wide – wide and purple-blue, like the seas is way south. And I've seen his white horses come in, with the blood streamin' free from their throats. And I've seen – him – stalkin' across the waters.'

The man dropped his face in his thin hands, and fell suddenly silent.

'Blair,' said the doctor patiently, 'I am following your story with full attention and belief. Understand that. But so far, except that you have told us where you found the box, I have learned practically nothing. Are you willing to answer a few questions?'

'Ask ahead, sir.'

'Then, first, what did you tell Mr Robinson that night when you visited him in his study?'

'Oh, that. Why I told him all I've told you and a bit more. I begins by explainin' to him that I'd made a big mistake sellin' the thing to that there dealer, Jacob Lutz. Yer see, when the dreams got too bad and I feels sure it's the box is bringin' 'em on me, I decides the best way is to get rid of it.

'He's been tellin' me he must have it back; but me, I reckons it's mine to sell, and the curse of it can pass to the man that buys. I'd tried to get it open and couldn't; and I didn't dasst break it.

'So I takes it to this feller Lutz and strings him with a yarn about how it had been stole from a temple in China, thinkin' he'd pay more fer it than if I let on I'd picked it up off a bare rock, where it was lyin' loose fer the first comer. He only give me three dollars at that, but I takes it fer reasons of my own and walks out of his shop, thinkin' myself a free man. Free! I'd oughter knowed better than traffic that way with his property. He come to me – he come that night – different –'

The sailor seemed to choke on the words and again covered his face.

'I think I understand,' assured Vanaman gently. 'Captain Porter, this man is sane, but he is speaking of a matter so far beyond my own comprehensions that I can't even attempt to explain it to you now. Let me talk it out with him, and if we appear to talk like madmen, have patience.'

'I'm having it,' Porter retorted rather grimly.

'Go on, Blair. You decided you must recover the box? Was that it?'

Blair drew a long breath and nodded.

'I went to Lutz and managed to dig old Robinson's address out of him by lettin' on I could tell his customer what the red inscription means. I dunno what it means. Unless it's his autygraft, wrote on the bottom to show who it belongs to. I didn't blow in on Robinson till near midnight, because I'd been havin' another bad spell with them wakin', walkin' dreams of red cities and the like. I tells Robinson fair what I'd been told in them dreams. How the box was buried ten – twenty thousand years ago; I dunno just how long, but before even the Bible was wrote. And how inside of it is big secrets – secrets he told to the rulers of the ten red cities. And how, me havin' stole it accidental-like, not knowin' who it belonged to, he's willin' I should give it back peaceable and no more trouble for me. And I offers Robinson the three dollars Lutz gimme fer it.

'Robinson sits there and laughs. Thinks I'm crazy, maybe. But he don't laugh long because – because the air begins to turn cold and damp and – and in at the door –'

The doctor interposed hastily, 'Never mind describing that, Blair. I've been through it myself sufficient times.'

'Well, Robinson has the box, and seein' as how he's come after it in person like, I don't think I'm needed any more around there. I jumps fer the winder, the door bein' occupied, slips and pulls down something that breaks with an awful crash. I come up with a chair in my grip, smashes at the winder, and jumps.

'That's the last I seen of Robinson fer three days, me not bein' interested to go round to his place inquirin', and the dreams lettin' up a bit, so I thinks, maybe I'm rid of my troubles fer good. Then I meets Robinson on the street. He's in his autymobile, and he calls me over and says he knows as much as me now. That I was right about him, but was a fool and quitter ter give in to him. Old Robinson says to me: "What I want I get, and what I get I keep. That's why I'm ridin' round in this here car while you and your weak, quittin' kind trudge it barefoot. There ain't nothin' can scare me. And as fer takin' the box from me, he can't do it. How do I know? 'Cause he's been tryin' almighty hard, and ain't done it. I aim to keep the box, 'cause I bought it and it's mine. Maybe I'll open it some day. Good-bye, Blair. Remember, quitters is losers!" And he druv off, laughing.

'After that the dreams came back worse than before, and I figure maybe I can steal the box and give it back to him. I hangs around, but not bein' bred nor trained a cracksman I don't know just how to go about it. Then I reads as how Lutz bought him a white horse and then killed himself instead of it. I knowed right away why he done it. So I tries the same stunt, thinkin' it might pacify him.

'It didn't do no good – no good at all. And my last five dollars was gone. I ain't et a thing in two days, sirs. I was hangin' around by the docks, thinkin' maybe I'd best end it like Lutz did, when old Robinson druv out on the wharf, where I was, in his car. I heered everything that passed. I dunno exactly why, but hearin' that tall feller talk I suspicioned what was in the wind.

'I might have spoke and warned old Robinson, I suppose. But somehow it seemed to me he had this comin' to him. Braggin' on how what he gets he keeps, and laughin' me out fer a quitter! And besides – now he's got the box back, maybe he'll let up on me.'

'Blair, I ask you again, and this time I wish a straight, definite answer; who is he?'

The man's lips twitched nervously. His vacant gaze wandered from the doctor's face to Porter's, then fixed on the open doorway.

'Dr Vanaman, sir, he has a lot of different names. He told me all of 'em, sir, and cursed me by each one. I'll tell yer the name they called him by in the ten red cities, but I don't just like ter say it out loud. He might hear, and think we was callin' him.'

Going close to the doctor, where he was seated by the chart-table, Blair bent and whispered a single word in his ear. Vanaman's expression of patient if strained attention did not change.

'I thought so,' he nodded. 'And when Lutz spoke of an archangel –'

'That's the name Lutz would choose to call him, sir, him bein' a Jew.'

'The "archangel of the abyss." Yes, I believe he is referred to by that name somewhere in the Old Testament. Queer – still, the idea of such a being might be translated under the name most familiar to the mind that received it. Now am I right, Blair, when I say that neither you nor Mr Robinson nor Jacob Lutz had any knowledge of the nature of the past history of the green box except what you learned through dreams?'

'That's right, sir.'

'And you have never been touched – never been physically harmed by any of the appearances you have seen in connection with it?'

'No, but –'

'Just a minute. What I am getting at is this. Until to-night, at least, every remarkable occurrence in connection with the green box has been of an hallucinatory character.

'That is, these five people – you and Lutz and Mr Robinson, and Miss Robinson and myself – yes, and my aunt, too; that's six – six of us have seen certain visions or illusions similar to those which a man might witness in delirium or insanity. The fact that all six of us have seen practically the same illusions makes it impossible to attribute them to mental aberration. The fact that none of us, so far as known, has suffered physical harm –'

'That man Lutz –'

'Was frightened into real madness. Lutz was not injured by an outside force. He took his own life. I say, the fact that none of us has been physically touched or harmed proves to my mind, at least, that behind those visions is no living, dreadful being seeking to reclaim the box as you fancy. On the other hand, the fact that we have all seen the same visions proves that behind them in a real, active agency of some kind.

'Now, and particularly since hearing your story, I believe the green box, which was cast up from the abyss is a memento of perhaps the most awe-inspiring event in the world's long life. In ancient days, before our written history began, there lay another continent between Europe and the two Americas. The Azores Islands are generally conceded to be crests of its submerged mountains. Through tradition, not history, its name has come down to us as Atlantis. There have been suppositions that the great Deluge recorded by the Hebrews, the Chaldeans, the Greeks, and in fact by the traditions of nations all over the world, including North and South America, refers to the destruction of Atlantis by earthquake, volcano, and flood.

'If we may at all trust the Greco-Egyptian legend as written by Plato, Atlantis was the center of very high civilization and its people may well have been the possessors of many arts and inventions whose secret was lost when the land perished. Also, they were worshippers of Poseidon, the sea god, who was supposed to have founded their government.

'Now, Blair, the vast, terrible being who haunts you is nothing – nothing, do you understand? Or rather, he is only a thought and idea – relic of an ancient religion dead long ago and revived in your mind by your temporary ownership of an object once surrounded by myriads of people who held the same belief. Those people are dead, as you say, these many thousand years. But the thing you found still radiates their ideas as thought-waves, reproduced much, as sound-waves are.

'That is my honest belief in respect to the green box, Blair. That enshrined in it is a secret, indeed – a secret of the ancient peoples, who were wiped from the earth when the cities of

Atlantis fell before earthquake and flood. The secret which our modern science has groped for, but not yet found – a device for recording and reproducing thought vibrations.'

Porter's brows were knit in a frown of perhaps excusable bewilderment, and as Blair's blank eyes met the doctor's the latter realized that his ingenious theorizing had been intelligently followed by no one save himself. Still, that he had evolved an explanation on material grounds to satisfy even himself meant a great deal to Dr Vanaman just then. He hurried on:

'What happened to-night – the abduction, I mean – can't be properly explained till we catch the abductors. I am absolutely sure, however, that they will prove mere human beings like ourselves, and it may even be that the kidnappers knew nothing about the green box. Mr Robinson has many enemies. He himself has confided that fact to me. He may have been kidnapped for ransom or in connection with some affair of which we are ignorant. Captain Porter, this man Blair is on the verge of collapse from privation. In common humanity, will you see that –'

'Message from the U. S. Destroyer Shelby, Sir.' A third time Mr Crosby's form blocked the doorway. He wore an expression of almost pleased anticipation, as if interested to observe his superior officer's probable reaction to the latest news. 'Near three hours ago the Shelby just missed collision with a big, black-painted sailing craft of some sort that tore by the Shelby's nose like the devil was behind her. Commander Jansen reports that he was on deck at the time and had a good view of her bow, with a big, bright-red dolphin curving out from it instead of a bowsprit. Says she was sail-rigged as near as he could make out, but with no canvas set, and going it under auxiliary power alone.

'The Shelby hailed, and tried to overhaul her. She was cruising without a glimmer of light, or a fog-gong or siren in action. Commander Jansen thought he'd like to speak a gentle word or so to her master. They lost her in the fog, though. That happened about five miles off Cape May.'

'And three hours ago!' Captain Porter's large fist smote the chart-table a resounding smash. 'Mr Crosby, I don't know what we are chasing! I've sat here listening to a yarn I can't make head or tail of till what with that and these crazy reports coming in it's all beginning to seem like a dream, and a bloomin' nightmare at that. I don't know if Red Dolphin is the Flying Dutchman or the devil's own private yacht; but whatever she is, I do know she's got my charterer aboard. And before the Lord, we'll hold on her trail so long as there's even a dream of a trail to hold!'

13.

In Pursuit of the Flying Dutchman

It was near midnight when Captain Porter expressed his bulldog resolve to 'hold on.' Dawn found the Nagaina waddling, still at half-speed, across the shifting, fog-obscured hills and valleys of the open Atlantic, well out from the Jersey coast. By his own request, the pilot had been dropped at Lewes, Delaware, and Captain Porter was again in personal command.

Those hours between midnight and dawn had been not without their own peculiar excitement. The destroyer Shelby was by no means the last vessel to sight Red Dolphin, as the stranger had been christened pro tempore. At intervals all night long the Nagaina's wireless apparatus had snapped and crackled acknowledgement of news, advice, and encouragement, some of it regrettably satirical, from fellow craft which had picked up earlier signals, and were many of them keeping in touch for mere gratification of the sporting instinct.

Unless some of these latter were also indulging a perverted sense of humor and sending in false reports, Red Dolphin had pursued her extraordinary course straight outward from Delaware Bay. A tramp steamer reported hailing a coastwise lumber schooner and receiving word of the stranger as a 'cursed fool running without lights and just missed taking our bo'sprit with her.'

The tug, Boston Beau, had also narrowly escaped collision with 'something big and black going at racing-boat clip. Not a light about her. Think saw red dolphin figurehead. Not sure. Too dark, going too fast.'

The revenue boat Kelpie not only sighted the stranger, but was now in irritated pursuit of her. The Shelby had been under orders, bound for Hampton Roads, but no such restriction hampered the revenue boat. Quite aside from Captain Porter's grievance, the Kelpie joined the chase as of a vessel recklessly breaking that ordinance which forbids any craft to careen through heavy fog, full speed, without lights, and silent.

In the consensus of all reports, one perhaps rather odd fact was noticeable. Wherever Red Dolphin had been encountered collision was escaped by a narrow margin; in each case she had flashed by, always crossing the other vessel's bow and always so close on that one or several persons aboard the endangered craft obtained at least a dim glimpse of her distinguishing characteristic, the scarlet, outcurving figurehead.

Had the stranger been intentionally bent on marking her course for pursuers, she could hardly have done better.

Another thing which Captain Porter noted with encouragement was an apparent slackening of that really incredible speed indicated by the earlier messages. Where by report the Nagaina had at one period been hours behind her quarry, at 3 a.m. Greenwich time the difference had abruptly lessened, and by the last report pursuer and pursued were separated by no more than twenty marine miles.

Dr Vanaman stood at the rail, peering outward with eyes that strove in vain to penetrate more than a rod or so through the blinding mist that still enveloped the steamer. From sheer necessity he had slept a couple of hours, flinging himself fully dressed on a cushioned transom in the saloon cabin. The rest had strengthened him, but his young, boyish face appeared unnaturally haggard as he strained his vision where the trained eyes of the lookouts were practically blinded.

Day was breaking and the fog had taken on a sulfurous, sickly hue. Mingling with it the black smoke from the Nagaina's funnels hung like a somber, writhing shadow above her wake, and all around her, so far as discernible, the waters appeared dark and ugly, as if a plowed field should be endowed with restless motion.

Despite the recent encouraging news, imparted to him by the

wireless man, Vanaman felt wearily, bitterly depressed. Presently his hand sought an inner coat pocket and brought forth a bulky envelope. From it he drew the folded sheets of what seemed a considerable manuscript.

It was, in fact, a very voluminous letter, written in the fine, careful hand of his eminent and scholarly acquaintance, Bowers Shelbach. The missive reached him the previous afternoon, but due to the peculiar stupor which had afflicted him all that day, he had then thrust it into his pocket without reading. Half an hour ago, awakening refreshed in the cabin, he had by mere chance discovered what was in his possession and perused with eager interest what might add a very important detail to his knowledge of the green casket. After reading, however, the eagerness had subsided to gloom.

Now he ran through the letter again, though with meager attention, for most of Shelbach's bulky epistle dealt with archaic linguistics in a technical manner not excessively interesting to a layman. It began with disquisition on certain analogies to the Aramaic or so-called 'Chaldee' in which portions of the Old Testament were originally written, and archaic Phoenician.

Dr Vanaman skipped with regrettable haste through not only this, but the equally careful and comparative analysis of each separate character in the traced inscription as submitted by the doctor. There followed a general summing-up from which one gathered that the characters represented either an erratic, mongrel dialect combining a Semitic root with Phoenician idiom, or – and here Shelbach became palpably earnest and enthusiastic – they might possibly represent a phonetically written language predating the known forms of Semitic, Phoenician and hieratic Egyptian.

To be certain, Professor Shelbach desired further data – very much desired them. In the sacred name of archeology he demanded to know whence Vanaman had obtained this inadequate fragment of ancient writing, and if there were more of it in existence why he had not copied the entire inscription and submitted that with full information as to the source from which he had derived it.

At the end Shelbach became almost accusatory over his friend's assumed neglect, urged him immediately to forward complete data, and signed his eminent name with an emphatic flourish. Not anywhere in the letter had he given the intelligible translation so much wished by Vanaman, but down in a corner of the last sheet, added as a considerate afterthought, the doctor found a pencil-scribbled postscript.

It consisted of two short phrases set in quotation-marks, and Vanaman judged they were meant for alternative translations of the inscription.

Moodily, he folded the letter and thrust it back in his pocket.

'To the great deep. To the abyss.'

Shelbach had been wrong in terming the inscription a 'fragment.' It was a complete, and – should he allow himself to so consider it – an ominous dedication. Unwillingly he canvassed in memory those qualities of the green casket which, quite aside from the 'dreams' it brought, had made it an enigmatic mystery.

There was the fact that no scratch nor mar nor finger-mark was retained by its lucent surface through one single instant after the experimenter's glance ceased to observe it. He had several times tested and proved that past even his materialistic doubts.

There was the occasional illusion of great depth beneath the clouded surface. Had the effect been invariable it would have seemed less troublesome to explain. But it was not invariable. There were times when one might turn the box as one would, trying all angles and degrees of light, and still see only a polished, blue-green surface. Other times when one's glance was caught unaware and drawn, sickened and entrapped, through an infinite green abyss.

There was the scarlet inscription itself, that consistently refused to remain in evidence, yet only sank or somehow translated itself to the bottom when the method of its queer maneuver could not be observed.

Summed up, Vanaman regretfully admitted that none of these eccentricities followed the known laws of material phenomena as applied to a solid object.

Water will endure the marks of no wounds nor fingerprints. The green sea is at times translucent and again blank, enigmatic surface. That which is laid across it may float there, or sink through the lucent depths beneath.

'To the great deep. To the abyss.'

Must he believe with the over-daring old tyrant who called the box his that its other dread claimant had an actual and sentient being? That the ocean possessed intelligent spirit, and could claim its dedicated own?

In any case, what might not the past night have meant to his maid of the moonlight hair? At the very best, she had been all these hours at the mercy of men God alone knew how unscrupulous. At the worst – Vanaman shuddered and turned from the rail. God alone knows just what strange powers He permits to exist behind the veil of palpable materiality that for most mortals seems the real and only world.

'That you, doctor? Bloomin' pea soup of a morning, eh? Come up here with me if you like. When the weather thins there's a chance that our Flying Dutchman may find us unpleasantly close.'

Porter was speaking over the bridge rail, and the doctor slowly ascended a nearby flight of wooden steps and joined him.

'Haven't heard from the Kelpie in quite a while,' continued Porter. 'Their operator's asleep, maybe. Or she's dropped the trail.'

'The fog seems thinning a bit.'

Vanaman's tone held a note of suddenly renewed hope and courage. Porter's blunt, powerful personality seemed to delete all weirdness from the chase; the Nagaina's master distinctly represented the sane, the solid, and the resolute. His ship was driving through the ghost-land, cleaving phantom mists that writhed to spectral forms in the wind of her passage; but Porter himself was a common, honest man, who hunted down other common men, not so honest. Though he spoke of Red Dolphin as the Flying Dutchman, that was purely in jest. Unlike the doctor, he had no faintest doubts of her solid, sane materiality of being.

And it was true that all around and above them the fog's impenetrable quality now stood further off, like close walls that withdrew themselves.

The Nagaina seemed moving at the center of a semi-globular clear space that moved with her; as if in a world of otherwise universal cloud one clear cavity existed and traveled as an immense air bubble might travel through water. On all sides the yellowish mist rose in an unbroken but continually shifting wall, that curved upward to a dome-shape and was thinner there, so that the light of a presumably clouded sky gleamed through it grayly. And beneath, dark as green-black ink, heaved the naked sea.

Came an abrupt shout from one of the lookouts forward.

Down in the engine-room a signal shrilled, and the stout old steamer shuddered from stem to stern as her reversed propellers churned the water to leaping geysers of foam. But the Nagaina was no light, easily controlled craft to stop or turn in her own length. Her clumsy bulk had plowed forward a good three hundred yards or more before coming at last to a quivering and reluctant halt.

Though Dr Vanaman had not seen what Porter's alert eyes had discerned even before the lookout's warning cry, he judged instantly that their quarry or some vessel resembling it had been sighted. Nowhere about them now, however, was there even a shadow in the mist to betray the presence of another ship.

Crosby had come running open-mouthed up the bridge-ladder, and giving no heed to the doctor's excited questions Porter shot a rapid order at his second and himself fairly plunged to the deck below, with a barked 'Come along!' over his shoulder that brought Vanaman plunging after him. The latter had but a confused idea of what might have happened or was about to be done; but prospect of any sort of action spurred his energies to eager life.

In the rush of haste which Porter seemed to consider necessary, it was not until several minutes later that the doctor acquired any definite knowledge of what they were about.

They were then aboard the Nagaina's launch, which had been filled with men, dropped to the water with man-of-war'sman speed and sent flying back along the steamer's still frothing wake.

'Red Dolphin is back along here somewhere, and she isn't moving. She's laid to!'

Porter made the announcement with a kind of fierce triumph that promised ill for the abductors of his charterer.

'Engine trouble, likely – and there isn't a breath of breeze for her sails. Before the Lord, doc, we've got her!'

The little party of eight men who had tumbled into the launch under their captain's hasty orders formed by no means so inadequate an attacking force as might have been expected from a peaceful vessel like the Nagaina.

Among the supplies put aboard by her first charterer had been a number of heavy caliber sealing rifles, intended for use against the large game of the north. Early in the pursuit, Porter had ordered these weapons broken from their cases, and had distributed them with ammunition among those of his crew whom be considered most reliable and cool-headed. There had been time nor opportunity for practise, but these eight men at least knew how to operate and fire the guns, and even in unpractised hands a sealing rifle is a formidable weapon.

Captain Porter, however, hardly anticipated an actual battle. He felt nearly sure that when the scoundrels aboard Red Dolphin found themselves facing a band of resolute, armed men, they would surrender, preferring a jail term to possible death by a soft-nose bullet.

Porter himself was armed only with the pistol he usually carried, and Dr Vanaman was not armed at all. The latter, however, had a motive even more powerful and aggressive than Porter's for wishing to come up with Red Dolphin, and was in a mood which made him probably the most dangerous man of the party.

As the launch sped onward, the seething rush of her passage across the dark, foam-laced swells, the throb of her engine and the hoarse hooting of the Nagaina's fog-siren behind them were the only sounds to be heard. If Red Dolphin were actually lying to near by, as the captain claimed, she was in no way advertising her position.

Except in heavy weather, a steamer's wake will lie like a frothing white path for a considerable time after her passage. As the most direct line back to that point from which Red Dolphin had been sighted, Porter headed straight by that path till he was certain he had overshot his mark. Then he began to circle. If, as he hoped, the quarry was lying helpless through engine trouble, sooner or later the agile, swift little launch must nose out her misty hiding place.

The air, heavy with moisture, was also very warm and breathlessly still. Several times Vanaman observed the captain glance upward and about him with a slight frown as of some trouble other than his anxiety to discover the kidnapper's vessel.

'Queer weather,' he muttered once. 'Bloomin' queer!' And presently he added loud, addressing the doctor: –

'Ever since we left the bay, we've been running through a low-pressure area. Now it's tightening up. Something's due to break soon, and I'll be hanged if I know exactly what. If we were in lower latitudes I'd say we were in for a bloomin' typhoon, but up here, and with this queer, warm fog –'

The sentence was abruptly cut in two by a shout from one of the men. 'Sail, 'o! Ship on the starboard bow, sir!'

The effect as of a semi-globular bubble of clear space which had surrounded the steamer, moved also with the launch. Looking where the man pointed, all saw a vague, enormous black bulk, looming, shadowlike, through the denser mist a hundred yards off to the left.

At a wave of Porter's hand, the steersman flung over the little wheel, and the launch swung sharply round toward the shadow.

The circular space of clear vision swung with her. The looming shadow, magnified by the mist, seemed to condense; at once growing smaller and more definite.

An instant later Porter again flung up his hand, this time with a cry in which amazement mingled with some emotion very like shocked terror.

'Stop her!' he shouted. 'Stop! For God's sake, what is this we've been chasing?'

14.

The Apparition

*Deep calleth unto deep at the noise of thy waterspouts;
all thy waves and thy billows have gone over me.'*

PS. XMII, 7.

The steady stuttering of the engine ceased, and the launch swerved so sharply as to come perilously near capsizing. For one moment, in fact, a frothing lip of water was actually flooding in over the submerged counter. Vanaman and all the others ranged along the port side were drenched from the waist down. The boat righted, however, and no one had even a thought to spare for their narrow escape from foundering.

The launch had come about broadside on to a vessel which there could be no doubt was Red Dolphin. Less than forty feet distant, the conspicuous figurehead curved out, bold and scarlet, at her prow.

But how had Captain Porter – how had any of the various persons who had caught glimpses of the ship failed even in the night and fog to perceive her utterly strange and inexplicable character?

Black she was, but not with the blackness of pigments. Rather it seemed that her ancient, crumbling timbers were darkened and rotted by an age too incredibly great for computation.

She was rigged, indeed, with sails. But for all her hundred foot length, the three masts stepped at stem, stern and amidships were mere slender spars – and spars, moreover, that had a broken, splintered appearance, as if each one of them had been blasted by many lightning strokes.

Her lack of a bowsprit had been noted by Shelby's commander, and Captain Porter had mentioned the odd 'swell out and curve-back cut' of her stem. But neither seemed to have taken the full sense of incongruity to a modern vessel presented by that swelling, curving, quaintly fashioned prow. And no one, apparently, had even glimpsed the equally quaint stern, with its extended post, elaborately carved though moldering, that curved inward above the strange, high poop.

Her auxiliary power – the means by which she had moved without spread of canvas – had not, it seemed, been provided by the gasoline engine or steam turbines which one would have naturally looked for in a vessel of her remarkable speed. Her actual mode of propulsion was now equally obvious and astounding. Down all her worm-eaten hundred feet of freeboard were cut three rows of apertures like oblong portholes. Out of these, one row above the other, extended three banks of oars, some two-score in all, long, heavy, and with that appearance of black, crumbling age that characterized the ship's timbers.

No sign of life was visible beyond her somber bulwark. The oars trailed without motion, save that imparted by the restless waters. She lay silent, as if deserted, rising and falling gently with the long, quiet heave of the ocean. She was a craft more strange than the Flying Dutchman of old fables. She was a rotting anachronism, a resurrection from ages infinitely remote.

In some cases a classical education gives advantage over even the widest practical experience. Mere landsman that he was, it was Vanaman, not Porter, who identified her type.

'A trireme!' His voice sounded hoarse and strange to him. 'A trireme galley of the cataphract Phoenician type, that preceded even the Greek. And by the look of those timbers she's as old as – Porter, Porter, man, what is that ship?'

'I don't know!' The bluff seaman's face was yellow-white under its tan. 'Look. Look over beyond there!

'What – ah – h!'

The exclamation as it came from the doctor's throat had a sound of awestruck recognition.

In one direction, that toward which Red Dolphin's prow was pointing, the mist had cleared yet further. Or rather, without clearing, it had become more transparent. Vanaman had an impression, real or fancied, that the foggy saturation of the air was no less, only some strange power was gradually robbing it of that refractive quality which makes it visible. To a certain distance one could see through it clearly; but there was an indefinable effect of gazing through transparent water rather than transparent air. For five hundred yards, at least, the peculiar clearness now extended; beyond that the eye could as yet penetrate but dimly.

What vast, mist-veiled shapes were those which loomed there? Buildings? Monumental outposts of some great harbor? But no land had been within fifty miles when they first came on Red Dolphin.

And these buildings, if buildings they were, glittered even through the enshrouding mists with a vivid and ominous color.

Scarlet they were, beyond doubt; scarlet as blood newly shed; scarlet as the writing that lay across what he claimed for his own.

Dr Vanaman felt a sickly weakness creeping over him; a helpless yielding to that fearful belief he had fought against.

There, close at hand, very ghastly because of its suggestion of incredible age, lay the rotting black galley. Obscurity was too swiftly dissolving from about certain habitations of man lately seen by several in dreams, but which in their material being lay sunk miles deep beneath green waters; deeper still in the mists of antiquity. And from far off, somewhere behind them, hooted the Nagaina's extremely modern steam-siren, as if in mournful but incongruous comment.

The eight armed men who had been brought to subdue Red Dolphin were, it may be supposed, no more imaginative nor easily frightened than the average. Yet meeting this strange end to the chase and perceiving also the indubitable dismay of their leaders, it is likely that with Porter's orders or without them the launch would have been put about and sent speeding away, save for one reason.

Over all, that feeling of tension which Porter had expressed as 'something due to break' was stealthily, steadily tightening its grip.

The men had probably no real wish to see more of red buildings that loomed where buildings of any kind or color had no right to be; their proximity to that strange, rotting black ship may well have excited the superstitious dread of the seamen.

Yet, through several long, agonizing minutes not a man in the launch moved or spoke. Any human act, any human sound, it seemed, might snap the tension and precipitate whatever vast, superhuman event impended.

The fog's transparency was now complete, and there, where no land should have been, rose a land very strange and beautiful.

Mirage – illusion – dream – whatsoever the vision's nature, it had the appearance at least of solid reality.

Far in the background the peaks of snowcapped mountains pierced a lowering sky. Between them and the sea, on the flattened crest of a foothill, lifted what seemed to be either a single great building or the domes and towers of many smaller ones, surrounded by a high, encircling wall. Though small in the distance, this walled fortress or city stood out distinctly as a painted miniature because of its color – blood-red against the green lower slopes of the mountains.

Down from it curved a white road that led to a broad stream of water, not a natural river, but a canal cut by human hands; it stretched straight as a ruled line between the sea and a valleylike gap in the distant mountain range. This canal was crossed in many places by massive bridges, high-curved, single-arched, and built of scarlet stone.

The broad plain it bisected, stretching to the right and left far as the eye could travel, was verdant and cultivated in many regular fields, surrounding small isolated dwellings and villages, and far to the right the scarlet heights of another walled, pinnacled city.

In the immediate foreground, where canal and sea were united, the land retreated in the shape of a great bay. This bay was lined with built-up terraces of red stone, out from which jutted many wharfs and docks. Its waters were not empty, but thronged with shipping of a type as anachronistic, though by no means so time-rotted, as the galley of the dolphin figurehead. Great triremes, with the shields of their warriors ranged glittering down the length of their bulwarks, shared the anchorage with ships of more peaceful appearance, merchant-vessels carved and gilded from stem to stern and of sails vari-hued as bright banners.

At the point of the nearer of two promontories which guarded the harbor waters stood a pillared palace or temple, either built of solid metal or coated with smoothly polished plates of it. The metal was also red.

At the point of the other promontory appeared, not a building, but an immense group of statuary. One towering white figure, forty feet in height at least, faced outward toward the sea. It was chiseled to the form of a man, nude, mighty muscled, with wind-blown hair and beard. The colossal hand gripped a trident, and the figure stood erect in a scarlet chariot drawn by six wild, white steeds, about whose plunging marble hoofs scarlet dolphins disported.

The sculptor had given such vigor and life to the group that as the seething green waters curled about its base the galloping horses seemed almost to be in motion, the figure's hair and beard to be torn by wild winds as its chariot raced across the waves.

And now all the air and the earth and the sea were shaken by a sound, low but terrible. It seemed to emanate from no special source, but to fill all space simultaneously. The lowering sky had assumed a sulfurish yellow cast. A faint wreath of vapor that overhung one of the snowcapped mountains grew suddenly dense, black, shot with forks of ruddy fire. It rolled down the mountainside, an avalanche of black cloud, and from the peak above an enormous flame burst skyward.

Yet still, save for that low, all pervading moan, and the hoot of the invisible steamer's siren, there was no sound.

The black cloud rolled on down the sides of the flaming mountain. It spread across the plain, engulfing the fields, the villages, and the dwellings. The hill which bore the nearest red city split asunder in awful crevasses that belched flame and smoke and closed again.

Throngs of little running figures fled across the plain, pursued, overtaken, and swallowed up by the rolling cloud. In the harbor, close at hand, crews of swarthy men sprang with feverish haste to run up the rainbow-hued sails of the merchant-vessels. The oarsmen of the war-galleys swarmed to their seats on the rowing-benches.

The actions of all were those of men stricken by fear to confusion and mad haste; yet, though so near, their shouts reached the men in the launch only as a faint, shrill piping, as if ere the sounds could be heard they must pierce some almost infinite distance of space – or time.

And now, out of the pillared scarlet palace that terminated the nearer promontory, there issued another sound, very faint, like the noise of men chanting far away. Two portals of red metal swung asunder, and in the aperture a single figure appeared. It was the form of a man, dressed in a flowing robe, gray-green in color, like the sea under gloomy skies. His face where it showed between flowing hair and beard was white as death's self. Aloft in his hands he bore something that gleamed greenly lucent, an oblong block of clouded emerald.

Very slowly he descended the temple steps, and after him followed many others, dressed like himself. Six of these followers held the scarlet-hued halters of six white stallions, that plunged and stumbled on the flight of broad, shallow stairs.

Chanting still – in those dim ghosts of voices – the group reached a platform of red stone some twenty feet above water-level, where they halted facing the opposite promontory with its colossal statue of the ocean deity.

The leader of the priests – if priests they were – now held the green thing aloft with one hand while with the other he gestured toward the nightmare of flame-shot smoke rolling from landward down upon the harbor.

The ghostly chanting had ceased and his single voice sounded thin and faint as the singing of air through a wind-harp. By his gestures, he made some invocation or plea to the statuesque sea-god across the harbor. The men in the ships had ceased their frantic exertions and wherever they chanced to be, in the rigging, at the oars or lined up along gaudily gilded bulwarks, they stood at gaze watching the priests as if fascinated.

The speaker's thin-voiced oration came to an end. Those behind him drew upon the blood-red halters, bringing the fierce white stallions to the red stone platform's edge. Six knives flashed simultaneously. The great horses fought, screaming and plunging. Four of the priests accomplished the sacrifice without harm to themselves; the other two were carried over the brink by the maddened, blood-streaming beasts they were slaughtering. No effort was made toward rescue. The main body of the priests had resumed their monotonous, piping chant.

Landward the black cloud from the mountain had overspread all the land, and above it not one peak, but three, were spouting flame to the skies. No sign of the red cities was now visible. Just those three flares, like torches of the awful and angered gods, and below them a rolling black wall that swept onward swiftly.

Then he who had held aloft the glittering green casket grew angered – or maddened. His voice shrilled out like the shriek of an angry sea-bird. Puny little creature that he was, with word and gesture he cursed alike the terrific cataclysm that was destroying the land and the great sea-god, whom prayer nor sacrifice had moved to avert it.

Raising the green casket yet higher, with all his force he flung it from him, so that it fell into the sea, midway between the two promontories.

A thin wail of terror rose from his companions; the seamen in the ships and the galleys wrung their hands.

The black cloud had now reached the scarlet terraces that surrounded the harbor. Towering hundreds of feet into the air, shot with forked lightnings and moving with a rolling motion, in another instant it must overwhelm the harbor and sweep outward across the sea.

Yet, though directly in its path, the men in the Nagaina's launch crouched motionless, either numbed by terror or held quiescent by that same nightmarish paralysis which had visited Vanaman in those bad nights he had previously passed on guard.

And as on each of those occasions the paralysis had been broken by old Robinson's scream for help, so this time also the evil charm lifted at a sound. It was not, however the voice of man nor beast, nor the deafening roar that in more normal cases accompanies volcanic activity.

Begun on a mournful, sobbing, gulping note, it crescendoed upward to a wail more weird than was ever produced by anything except that particularly weird and modern invention, the steam siren.

Every man aboard the launch started as if galvanized to a new lease of life. They had been hearing that sound at intervals ever since leaving the steamer, but muffled by fog and distance. Now it was close at hand. If their sense of direction were not utterly at fault, it came from the very midst of the towering black cloud that threatened.

Another instant and out of the cloud's midst at sea-level, sweeping with no apparent hindrance straight through the scarlet terraces and antique shipping, the Nagaina plowed incongruously into view.

She was greeted by a feeble cheer from the launch. As a great, clumsy reality might rend asunder and dissipate a mirage, so the steamer's coming had banished the vision of doom. In one brief flash of time the false transparency of the fog was gone. The circle of clear vision narrowed again to a bare fifty-yard radius. There was no red temple with despairing priests. There was no vast statue of an implacable ocean god. There was neither harbor nor lightning-shot cloud rolling down upon them.

Only the clumsy old steamer with propellers threshing the sea to foam as she came to a reluctant halt, the launch and the rotting black trireme with its dolphin figurehead. That last had not vanished. That was no mirage. That was real, or at least material in some sense, or it must have gone with the rest of the vision.

In the launch Vanaman sprang to his feet.

'Put me aboard that vessel!' he cried fiercely. 'No matter what damnable magic is about, there is the ship we've been hunting! Run the launch alongside, and put me aboard!'

Human courage, save when spurred by the all-powerful motive which actuated Vanaman, has a limit, and it is very likely that even if Captain Porter had dared comply with his passenger's demand, the men under him would have mutinied, rather than run any closer to Red Dolphin. The question of their courage, however, was not then put to test.

Even as the demand left Vanaman's lips a strange change overswept the ancient trireme; a shocking change, if there be shock in witnessing a revivification of a rotting corpse; in seeing a dead ship come to life. Apparently deserted as the trireme had been, its decks were suddenly aswarm with moving figures. The triple banks of oars that had trailed lax to the tide, lifted, came into alignment, and swept forward, feathering the waves in perfect unison. They took the water with a tearing, rushing sound, and like a spurred horse the black galley leaped forward.

A cry, inarticulate and heart-broken, burst from Vanaman's lips. It was echoed by a woman's voice from somewhere beyond the galley's near bulwark.

Two struggling figures came into view. One was tall, bearded, and clad in a flowing, grayish-green cloak; it bore, in fact, a startling resemblance to the figure of the priest in the vision. The other –

Again Vanaman shouted, and would have flung himself into the sea in a mad attempt to swim after the retreating galley had not Porter's strong arms closed about him and pulled him backward.

Struggling savagely, he yet realized a certain peculiarity in that struggle going on beyond the galley's bulwark. The woman – for the second form was beyond doubt Leilah – was not fighting as he had at first imagined to fling herself overboard from the nightmare vessel that had abducted her. On the contrary, she seemed to be straining every nerve and muscle of her frail young body to fight back from the bulwark.

With sharp abruptness the struggle ended. The gray-cloaked man had lifted the woman bodily. For a moment, as the man in the vision had elevated the phantom of the green casket, he held her high in his arms. Then he flung her outward, and with such superhuman strength that her body struck the water well beyond the foaming and perilous path of the oars.

In one great effort Vanaman had wrenched from Porter's grasp. Calm reasoning would have informed him that the quickest, safest way to rescue Leilah was by remaining aboard the launch, which could reach the spot where the woman had gone under far more quickly than any man could swim there. At that moment, however, the doctor was not in a mood for calm reasoning. The primitive, personal form of rescue was the only one that appealed to him, and not even pausing to remove coat or shoes, he plunged headlong overboard.

Reckless and condemnable though his act might have been under other circumstances, in this case it proved justified. Beyond doubt, the launch should have sped instantly to the rescue of the woman so ruthlessly jettisoned by Red Dolphin. As a matter of fact, it did nothing of the sort. Swimming with long, powerful strokes, the man in the water had reached his objective point, dived and come to the surface triumphantly bringing the woman's slim, limp form up with him, and still the launch had not moved a foot from its original position.

Vanaman was a strong man and a good swimmer, but hampered and dragged under by his clothing he now found it hard indeed to keep the woman's head and his own above water. Leilah herself made no struggle. Dead or living she was wholly insensible, a fact for which her rescuer was instinctively grateful, though without thought.

All that happened had taken place in a very brief space of time, too crowded with action and incident for coherent thought be possible. As their two heads rose on heaving shoulder of a swell, the black ship, though moving with increasing speed, was not yet engulfed by the surrounding mists. The steamer had barely lost way, and indeed was still sliding forward at a rate which promised to run Vanaman and his burden under in a few more seconds. And, aboard the launch, in the brief glance he had for it, there appeared to be some sort of battle going forward, accompanied by a burst of angry shouting.

The next wave went over Vanaman's head. Fighting desperately, he reached the surface a second time. He could not remain there long, but enough for one deep breath and a confused glimpse of some tremendous happening – a happening so great and terrible that afterward he might have believed it a figment of drowning delirium, save that the memory was confirmed by others who were not drowning and retained at least some measure of comprehension.

The universal breathless tension in the atmosphere had been by no means dissipated when the mirage-like vision of the red harbor faded. Captain Porter had previously referred to an area of barometric low pressure through which his vessel had been running since leaving the coast, and had also complained of the unnatural and wholly unforecastable state of the weather.

What now took place was actually as alien to the latitude as to the commonly known laws of meteorology. In the ordinary course of events, and with the given condition of warm, motionless, fog-saturated air, it could not have occurred. Let this be clearly granted, and the alleged fact that it did nevertheless occur may be accepted or denied as one has faith in the claims of those who witnessed the phenomenon. If it be accepted, the incident perhaps carried more weight as evidence of some supernormal power involved than any other of those very queer happenings which surrounded the advent and passing of the emerald casket.

When Vanaman, with his unconscious burden, fought his way to the surface that second time, he found himself caught in a rushing swirl of water which in the first brief second he believed to be caused by the Nagaina's advancing prow. The steamer did indeed loom close upon him, but the powerful impulse imparted to the water was sucking him not toward but away from her. The launch seemed also to be affected. Like a cork flung into a whirlpool's edge it gyrated, turned once completely around, then darted off with the tugging pull of the current.

Red Dolphin was still faintly visible as a receding shadow. The rush of current set dead in that direction. It was as if somewhere about or beyond the black galley a center of suction had been formed which affected not only the water, but the air, for in the brief while that Vanaman had been completely submerged a sudden wind had arisen. With appalling swiftness the wind became a gale, and the gale a tornado. On the loud, invisible wings of it the fog swept by, riven to trailing shreds and mingled with flying foam. The low, all-pervading moan that had begun some minutes earlier and persisted continuously now swelled to a deafening roar.

The upper clouds, visible at last, rolled low and unbroken save near the eastern horizon, where a single strip of clear blue-white lay like a rent slashed asunder in a night-black roof, and silhouetted against that one slash of light the ancient trireme was tearing along at a pace that seemed to make her strangely, frightfully at one with the dark, wild scene. As the spume and fragmentary mist wraiths scudded with the gale, so Red Dolphin fled across the wind-flattened billows, the path of her many oars a welter of spouting foam.

Specter? Ghost-ship? In good earnest the 'devil's own private yacht' that Porter had half-jestingly termed her?

Whatever she was, another moment saw her blotted from human vision.

Between Red Dolphin and the steamer a towering blackness roared upward toward the clouds. The clouds themselves had already dipped to meet it. Whirling, cyclonic, the dark upper vapors descended in a vast cone shape. The tip joined the raging cone of black water beneath; the powers of the air had mated in thunder with the ocean, and as one monstrous being stalked across the groaning abyss. Deep had called to deep, and the waterspout was born.

Caught in the racing current that drew them toward it, two tiny human atoms were borne forward, suffocated, drowning.

Yet through the chaos which filled his ears, through the roar of elemental forces mingled with a ringing as of shrill bells aclamor within his brain, the man thought that a human voice shrieked articulate words. Piercing as a seabird's cry, it seemed to drift down-wind from somewhere behind and above him. In one swift-passing flash of comprehension he knew that what he now beheld was the full physical, material form of that being whose phantom shape had haunted the green box; and also the human voice gave a name to it – the name of a very ancient god.

Then something struck him a heavy blow on the head, and oblivion with its blank, perfect peace closed over him.

15.

Claimed!

It is rarely indeed that the mind of any man is exposed to the full shock of a great event or catastrophe. Fear is necessarily limited by the powers of perception and imagination. In the face of an event too monstrous, imagination grows numb, perception halts, and the mind is shut in, as it were, by a protecting cyst of sheer incomprehension.

The crew of the Nagaina's launch had been afraid of the rotting black ship and the inexplicable vision that followed their discovery of it. When the woman was flung from its deck and Captain Porter issued an order – as he promptly did – that the launch go to her rescue, the men realized only that whatever or whoever had fallen into the water had been jettisoned by a craft for which they entertained the liveliest superstitious horror.

They wanted nothing to do with Red Dolphin's castaway, and when their commander would have himself started the launch in that direction, they turned on him to a man. Porter's type of courage being other than theirs, he insisted, using his fists for argument, and so started a fight much hampered by the cramped space it took place in and which ended within forty seconds of its beginning.

It ended because at that point the affair of the green casket approached its really terrible climax, and the cause for fear became so actual and great that the capacity for that emotion was numbed – paralyzed, as by a heavy blow.

When the launch spun about and shot off with the vortex current, Porter flung himself on the motor controls unhindered.

He was again captain, and the men obeyed what orders he chose to yell at them without a thought of rebellion.

Besides Captain Porter and Vanaman two other persons had retained their sense of responsibility and powers of independent action. One of these stood on the steamer's bridge, where more by instinct than accurate knowledge of the danger, ere the waterspout had half-formed, Mr Crosby had rung for full speed astern, and set the steamer ponderously back.

The other was James Blair. Perhaps through familiarity with terror, the latter retained presence of mind enough to unfasten and throw a life-preserver toward the drowning pair in the water. He was standing by the rail well forward, and the gale helped carry not only his voice, but the cork-jacket. So it was that Vanaman heard him shout and almost simultaneously was stunned by a missile meant to save his life, not destroy it.

Fortunately, as he went helplessly under, still gripping Leilah with one arm, he flung the other upward, and when the launch reached them not only the cork-jacket, but a limp hand tangled in its lacing-cords was still at the rushing flood's surface.

Danger from the waterspout was already over. Though it had formed so perilously near, in its full shape the cyclonic monster had swept off on Red Dolphin's track, leaving the steamer, launch, and swimmer to the ordinary perils of wind and wave.

Some hours passed, however, storm and waterspout were but memories, and the Nagaina well on her homeward course before Vanaman learned how it came about that he or any of those who set out to capture Red Dolphin had survived the attempt.

On first recovering consciousness his sole concern had been for his woman of the moonlight hair. Finding himself alive and snugly abed in one of the steamer's staterooms, he had refused to accept the steward's assurance that Miss Robinson also was safe aboard and had, in fact, regained consciousness long before he did. The only terms on which he could believe her alive after the terrific ordeal of that morning were those of actually seeing her and hearing her speak.

Against all protest he rose, dressed, and staggeringly, with the steward's shoulder to lean on, made exit from his stateroom.

Half-way across the saloon cabin he met the object of his solicitude, who had also risen, dressed, and come out, as he discovered afterward, bound on an errand remarkably similar to his own. The steward was a discreet and sympathetic man. Deciding that Dr Vanaman's need of his aid and support was ended, he retired, closing the door behind him.

Leilah made no effort to withdraw her frail little hands from the strong ones that gripped them both. She was rather pale, the slate-gray eyes were very large and dark, but otherwise she appeared her usual quiet, well-controlled self. Till she tried to speak.

'They told me – what you did,' came a tremulous whisper. 'It was – like you!'

And then Vanaman realized that for all her self-contained appearance, the woman was swaying, as she stood, with weakness and too-hardly repressed emotion.

Quite naturally his arms went about her and half-carried her to the cushioned transom near by. He sat down by her, and also quite naturally, her moonlight crowned head somehow found its way to his shoulder, and Leilah, the brave and self-possessed, gave way to a fit of crying that probably saved her reason.

She had been at too-close quarters with fear. Loyal faithfulness had involved her in an adventure too appalling. After a time she sobbed out parts of the story in fragmentary sentences, but neither then nor later did Vanaman learn all its details, nor did he wish to. A story like that is better forgotten as an evil dream than testified to in detail.

From the relation, however, broken as it was, he gathered that after leaving the wharf at Tremont, Leilah had been frightened – so frightened that though she tried to answer Vanaman who was calling her name through the fog, she had been able to make no sound above a whisper. This fright, however, seemed to have been purely instinctive. She had no true mental appreciation of its cause till the boat came alongside Red Dolphin.

'They carried us aboard that terrible old ship,' she sobbed. 'Uncle seemed to understand better than I what was happening.

'He said to me once: "He's got us a way I didn't expect, Leilah, but hold steady." And I tried to. Oh, I tried!'

'You would,' commented the doctor softly. 'But don't tire yourself telling me any more now.'

'I must! You must know everything, and help me decide what to do. I am not hurt – only frightened a little – but Uncle Jesse is still on that dreadful ship!'

Vanaman started, and an unpleasant chill crept down his spinal column. His own object in eagerly pursuing Red Dolphin had been achieved. Leilah safe, he had somehow taken it for granted that the uncanny vessel and the green casket and the tyrannical old hawk who had for once dared too much were all done with, so far as he and the woman were concerned.

Her words acted as an awakening shock. She loved that cruel, selfish old man, or at least had a loyal affection for him. If her Uncle Jesse was still living, or if there was any chance that he might be, Leilah would never rest till his rescue had been accomplished.

Clearly, then, the pursuit of Red Dolphin was not ended. The thought was far from pleasant, but Vanaman strove nobly to drag himself up to the Robinson ideal of never under any circumstances quitting.

'Tell me everything,' he said grimly, 'and if there's any way to do it I'll get him back for you.'

The story rambled on, sketchy and hard to follow, but convincing the doctor more firmly each moment that if he was to keep his word and attempt renewing Red Dolphin's acquaintance the adventure would involve more heroism than he had ever needed for any other act in his life.

She told of being escorted to an unlighted cabin in the dark of a ship that after the tender's return carried not a light in all its length. The cabin, as she and her uncle ascertained by feeling about, was bare of furnishings, and its walls, door, and floor had a strange, damp, soft feeling.

'All wet and spongy,' Leilah emphasized. 'I hated even to stand on it. And it smelled of old seaweed.'

For an unmeasured period they were left shut in this black hole. The ship rocked slightly from time to time. There was a steady, muffled roar as of rushing waters cloven at incredible speed. Then this noise lessened, ceased, and the rocking changed to a long, easy heave, as if the vessel had reached open sea and was either moving very slowly or lying at rest there.

Presently the cabin door opened and closed again. They knew that some one had entered, though the place being pitch black it was impossible for them to guess what sort of being was visiting them.

When the silent suspense grew intolerable, old Robinson flung a question into the dark.

It was answered by a voice which Leilah at first believed to be that of the tall man who had called himself captain. Later she was not so sure. Some of the time, she asserted, it seemed to be a human voice speaking in clear, resonant English; then again it would trail off into sounds that were not human.

'Murmurings,' she said, 'and long, liquid, rhythmic noises, like waves sweeping in over flat beaches. They would begin very low, and grow louder, and fall away again, and then merge back into the voice speaking. All the while one knew that what spoke in words and what caused the flowing noises was – was one – person.

'It was very terrible, there in the dark. I can't remember everything the – person told us. At first there was a good deal I couldn't understand. The words were all clear, and spoken in English, but the meaning seemed to pass through one's mind and leave hardly a memory. I think it was something about a world where there was no land, but only the green ocean rolling – from pole to pole. And how the land was born of the sea, and life came to it from the sea – I recall one sentence. "Because I am older than life – because all the life that is was created within me – I in my own being am also alive."

'Uncle and I stood over against the far wall, listening. Once I tried to take his hand. He had them both clasped tight around the bag that held the green box. He whispered: "Hold steady, girl. Stick by me, and hold steady!"'

The voice continued, growing more comprehensible and telling of lands that rose, were molded by fire and water, and taken again by the sea: 'Till one great land being risen from the abyss, men were born thereon and knew me as their father and worshiped me with obedience and sacrifice.'

The land was divided by the sea into ten great islands, each a kingdom, and the ten kings thereof called themselves sons of the sea and 'were as gods above their fellows.'

So passed many long ages. Other lands arose and other races were born, but 'they, my earliest children, still ruled all. They had much wisdom of me; they built them palaces of scarlet stone and of the red metal called orichalcum that was in no other place but the ten kingdoms. Wisdom went out then, enriching the world. They had art of letters, of the building of ships and of war. Greatest of all they possessed knowledge whereby every other race in the world was subject to and enslaved by them. Not alone the races of men, but the races of elemental spiritual beings who existed in chaos before life took its fleshly form. The powers of the air were their servants, and those vast demon forces that dwell in earth's fiery heart.

'And all this they had from me, because they were my children, and I loved them.'

The highest secrets were inscribed upon tablets of the scarlet orichalcum and kept in a sacred receptacle, 'which also they had from me, as a pledge of my love. Fire might not harm it, nor might it in any way be destroyed. Thus the secret knowledge was kept by the ten kings, descendants of my first sons, who only had access to it. Till drinking too deep of power and ease and wealth, they grew drunken and presumptuous. Content no more to name themselves sons of a god, they forgot their mortality of flesh and believed themselves gods indeed.

'They disclaimed their debt of love. They turned against me and would have enslaved me also by the secret words of power I had taught them. Then I knew that I had done wrong, for men are small and foolish, not worthy of so great power nor fitted to wield it. In my anger I rocked the earth. It opened beneath their cities. The eternal fires were disturbed and burst forth from the mountains.

'The greatest of the kings in that day was named Azaes. In his keeping were the written words of power which he and his brethren would have used to subject me.

'Perceiving the evil that presumption had brought on the kingdoms, he offered atonement and worship. But I was angry. The repentance and the sacrifice were vain. He cursed me then, and flung back my gift of high secrets. It was well. Men are small and of mortal flesh, They are not fitted to wield the power of the gods.

'The ten kingdoms ceased to be. My white horses ran where the heights of their mountains had lifted. I was weary of men, and slept. Till stirring in a dream it came to me that the sacred thing flung away by Azaes was again in the hands of a mortal. Give it me now, that I may rest and once more forget your race and its ingratitudes.'

Here the voice subsided again into murmurous wave noises, and from that to silence. For a long time there was no sound in the cabin save the breathing of the two human beings prisoned there and the beating of their hearts. The voice at last spoke again.

'You have shielded yourself against me with a strong shield – the devotion of two souls greater and purer than yours. But only one of them stands beside you now, and that one may not avail. Nor shall the noble be sacrificed with the ignoble. Presently you shall stand alone against me, and thereafter – your lone will against mine!'

The doors opened and closed, and the two humans were once more alone.

'And Uncle Jesse wouldn't say anything, except to tell me again that I must help him by holding steady, and that he was nearly sure even yet that he couldn't take the box nor do any violence to us unless we weakened. But he was wrong,' sobbed Leilah. 'After a while the tall man – the captain – came and opened the door. It was daylight outside. I could see him. I knew that he was not the one who had come and talked to us in the dark, but he looked so strange – like a – like a dead man.'

'No more!' pleaded Vanaman.

'I must finish. He didn't touch my uncle, but he took hold of me and dragged me away. Uncle Jesse just stood there, swearing, and holding the thing be wouldn't give up.

'I was carried up a flight of steps to a kind of high deck. Everywhere the wood of the ship looked as it had felt in the cabin. It was slimy, black-soft-looking. When I struggled free for a minute, my feet sank into the deck as if it was rotten with age. I looked down into the ship. There was a kind of narrow platform along the center. On each side of it were three rows of seats one above the other. The shafts of the oars thrust in over them, and there was one man at each oar. I call them men – they seemed to be alive – but their faces – I never saw a drowned body, but I've heard that after one has been in the water a few days its face –'

'Forget that part!' insisted Vanaman almost fiercely. 'You mustn't dwell on such memories. Try to think of them as a bad dream, and forget.'

'I'll try,' she conceded. 'At the time I wasn't so much afraid of the ship or crew, as I was of being taken, away from Uncle Jesse. I knew he needed me, and in the struggle I had grown too excited to be much afraid. Then I saw the steamer lying a little way off, and screamed, thinking help might be sent to us. I fought hard to get back to uncle, but the captain picked me up and – and threw me overboard, I suppose. After he lifted me from the deck I don't remember any more till I woke up in the stateroom that had been made ready for poor Uncle Jesse aboard here. And now, what are we going to do?'

'Save your uncle, if he can be saved. I've ceased trying to explain the affair on any grounds. But if we caught Red Dolphin once we can probably do it again, and if you were brave enough to fight against being dropped off that ship, I guess I've got the courage to go aboard it. I'll find Porter now and lay the case before him.'

'You are – good!'

They had both risen and stood facing one another. For some reason, the Robinson millions seemed very small, far away, and unimportant just then. Looking into that lovely, upturned face, Vanaman came perilously near forgetting the millions and explaining to their probable heir just exactly why he would risk his life, or his soul, or any other trifle in his possession to rescue a man he despised from a fate he had brought on himself.

By a great effort, he overcame the impulse and turned away with only a word or so, advising her to lie down and rest while he interviewed the captain.

Porter seemed rather surprised to see him on his feet again so soon, but was also glad of the chance to talk over recent events with a man who at least knew more of their causes than he did.

The two repaired to the chart-room's convenient privacy, and there the doctor frankly and fully laid bare all those facts concerning the green box with which Porter was not already familiar.

'The only thing to be done,' he said in conclusion, 'is to try and trace Red Dolphin as we did before – by wireless.'

Porter's weather-beaten face had remained gravely inscrutable throughout the narrative. Now a flash of some emotion flickered across it. 'Wait here a minute.'

He paused outside and was back shortly, carrying something that he flung down on the table. Then he wiped his hands, as if from some distasteful contact.

'By that,' he said slowly, 'I judge it won't be worth while to attempt any further tracing of Red Dolphin.'

The thing he had flung down was a fragment of wood, or

what had once been wood. There were some rotted indications of carving on it. Sponge-soft, slimy, and water-soaked, it might have been riven from some ancient wreck, lain lost for ages in the black ooze at sea-bottom.

'Don't ask me how wood in the condition of that stuff could float,' Porter continued. 'All I know is, it's a bit off Red Dolphin's stem, and there were a lot of other scraps like it drifting around when the storm blew over. I picked this one up just to make sure what it was, and kept it to show you. Now I've shown it to you, it's going overboard. Believe me, doctor, I've had enough of Red Dolphin, whole or in pieces. As for my charterer and his precious green box, I say this:

'If that story you've told me is true – I believe it – then I admire Mr Robinson's nerve, but I can't admire his judgement. He set himself against a power just one step lower than that of the Almighty. What? Oh, yes, I can believe that the big fellow out there' – he waved his hand in a sweeping, significant gesture – 'has a life and will of his own. If you'd spent most of your life in his company, like Blair and me, you wouldn't be so slow to believe it yourself, doctor. Come out on deck. I'd sooner keep a drowned body aboard than this bit of his ship.'

Gingerly he again raised the rotted fragment and the doctor followed him in silence to the taffrail. Flung far out, the fragment was instantly lost in the boiling wake.

'I like Robinson's nerve!' repeated Porter solemnly.

Astern the foaming wake stretched eastward across a field of lucent green, where a clear sun struck the following host of wave-crests to dazzling whiteness.

'At least,' the doctor said abruptly, 'we are no pagan worshipers to sacrifice white horses to Poseidon. If the secrets of lost Atlantis were enshrined in that casket –'

'It was God's will that they be returned to the abyss,' finished Porter.

The doctor made no reply. His mind had strayed from the weary mystery that had kept him in torment for a week to wonder exactly how this final news of her avuncular relative would affect Leilah – and himself. The old hawk was dead now, and his niece presumably a very wealthy woman in her own right.

Fortune-hunter! Wasn't it after all a kind of quitter's cowardice to place dread of the world's empty opinion above the most sacred and beautiful happiness a man may win to?

Suddenly, savagely he smote the rail with his fist.

'"What I want I get, and what I get I keep!"'

'Eh?' cried Porter, startled.

The doctor turned on him, his brown eyes very bright and resolute.

'That was old Robinson's motto,' he explained. 'It carried him too far and to his grave. But, believe me, Captain Porter, applied in the right way, it's a motto worth having! I'll take it as my legacy from a man who surely owed me one. I'm going below. See you later.'

A straight, fine-looking, good and resolute man, he swung off toward the main companionway. Like the dread being who had recovered the green casket, he meant to claim his own.

PENGUIN WEIRD FICTION

ANCIENT SORCERIES: THE ADVENTURES OF JOHN SILENCE
ALGERNON BLACKWOOD

Welcome to the casebook of Dr John Silence, Physician Extraordinary. After long and severe training – five years he was gone from the face of the earth, travelling who knows where – Silence returned to England as the greatest occult detective of the age. When he takes up an investigation, when he comes to the aid of some poor, frightened soul, you can be sure it will lead to the most strange and terrifying of circumstances: from pagan magic in remote France to battles with ancient Egyptian fire spirits, and from geometry-defying alternate dimensions to the most macabre of haunted houses.

Some of the first works written by Algernon Blackwood – one of the twentieth century's ghost story writers – these John Silence tales are a visionary blend of horror, fantasy and science fiction, and remain today as some of pinnacle achievements of weird fiction.

'Algernon Blackwood's stories chill the blood'

Guardian

WWW.PENGUIN.CO.UK

Penguin Weird Fiction

THE HOUSE ON THE BORDERLAND
WILLIAM HOPE HODGSON

A manuscript is found: filled with small, precise writing and smelling of pit-water, it tells the story of an old recluse and his strange home – and its even stranger, jade-green double, seen by that old man on an otherworldly plain where gigantic gods and monsters roam. Soon his earthly abode is no less terrible than this strange vision, as swine-like creatures boil from a cavern beneath the ground and besiege it. But a still greater horror will face the recluse – more merciless and awful than any creature that can be fought or killed.

The House on the Borderland, William Hope Hodgson's great masterpiece of cosmic fear, is an extraordinary novel that defied all accepted conventions of horror writing, forging in an instant a new, weird direction for the form.

> '**Forget vampires and gore . . . this is where the screaming really starts, out in the void, with no one left to hear**'
>
> Terry Pratchett

Penguin Weird Fiction

THE KING IN YELLOW
ROBERT W. CHAMBERS

Shot through with an unutterable sense of mystery, paranoia and dread, *The King in Yellow* is a linked collection of stories that swirl around a single motif: a terrible book that prompts an obsessive madness in all who look upon its pages. From a dystopian New York to the streets of Paris, these narratives offer glimpses and hints of impossible, terrifying revelations. Who is the King in Yellow? What is the Yellow Sign? And where might be that ancient and famous city, Carcosa?

Combining expectation-defying horror with decadent description, *The King in Yellow* has proven to be one of the most durable and brilliant collections of weird fiction ever written, inspiring countless authors, from the mythos of H. P. Lovecraft to the fantasy worlds of George R. R. Martin.

'A classic . . . a fantastic collection of short stories'

Guardian

WWW.PENGUIN.CO.UK

Penguin Weird Fiction

WEIRD FICTION: AN ANTHOLOGY

Sometime around the turn of the twentieth century, something happened, something . . . weird. In the dark halls of ivy-clad manors, in the ancient woodland escapes of New England, a generation of authors was inspired to radically reinterpret the horror and fantasy writing of the past. From the terrible plagues of Edgar Allen Poe to the religious terror of May Sinclair and on to the awful, tentacle-faced mythos of H. P. Lovecraft, this anthology celebrates the very best of this writing, a collection of brilliant tales that for generations have delighted and horrified.

> 'Escape from the prison-house of the known and the real into those enchanted lands of incredible adventure and infinite possibilities which dreams open up to us, and which things like deep woods, fantastic urban towers and flaming sunsets momentarily suggest . . .'
>
> H. P. Lovecraft